Girl on the Se

& other stories

Too thin to cover.

John F Bennett

Girl on the Seventh Floor
and other stories

JoFra Press

The following stories, collected into one volume for the first time, were written between 1972 and 1986, mostly during the earlier period. No attempt has been made to adapt them to the present time.

First published 2018
©John F Bennett 2018
Re-printing January 2019
Second amended edition 2019

The story *Girl on the Seventh Floor* was first published in
Short Stories Magazine October 1981

Printed and bound in Great Britain by PurePrint Group
Crowson House, Bolton Close, Uckfield,
East Sussex, TN22 1PH
Tel +44 (0) 1825 768811
Fax +44 (0) 1825 768062

ISBN 978-1-5272-2033-1

Cover picture: ©John F Bennett 2018

JoFra Press
PO Box 40, Bexhill TN40 1GX
www.jofrapress.co.uk
publisher@jofrapress.co.uk

Dedicated to Moya Bennett

Contents

Girl on the Seventh Floor

Smudge pulled the lift handle out from the wall and leant his weight on it; the numbers ground past the grill: 6, 7.

'Er, young man!'

Smudge looked round at the prosperous looking, fur-decked, lady who had spoken. She was pulling her stole around her as if to protect herself against him.

'I did say sixth floor young man.'

'You din' say nuffin'.'

'Well what do you do when someone doesn't tell you? Do you not ask?'

'No, I take 'em to the nine.'

'Well kindly just take me to the sixth floor young man and quickly.'

Smudge brought the lever back to a central position and then slowly brought it back, out and then down. The lift started to descend. He knew that when the 7 was half way up the grill door he should slowly begin to release the handle. Instead he let the lift speed on so that when it did come to rest at the sixth floor it did so with a suddenness which shook the whole cage and sent the fur-draped lady crashing against the wall.

'Sorry,' he said with a smirk.

She stood with dignity while he opened the gates with the lever, and walked out without looking at him. Then she turned and shouted back:

'Do you realise that I am the wife of Mr Grayson?'

'Poor ol' Mr Grayson!' Smudge said.

'And that he can have you sacked?'

'He ain't important.' (Smudge knew his hierarchy. All the messengers and lift men knew their hierarchy).

She stormed off with a shiver of furs like an angry rabbit, saying: 'I'll be back in a moment.'

'Silly cow,' Smudge muttered, and carried on up to the ninth. He knew the other lift men would be there because, as long as you stayed on the ninth, nobody knew where you were and, once you moved down for a passenger, you could be going up and down all day with the other two lifts on the ninth floor. One of the lift-men had tried the dodge of stopping in between floors once, but that trick was short-lived: someone had noticed he wasn't on the ninth, first or basement and that he wasn't picking up passengers. He wondered just where he was and, fearing some accident, called in the lift mechanic. When Charlie Byrd was found smoking happily between the seventh and eighth floors, he was taken to the Head Messenger's department.

'Charlie you're a bloody idiot.'

'I was only...'

'Smoking in the bloody lift for a bloody start. Bloody suicide.'

'But...'

'And not working. I don't bloody blame you for not bloody working - it's letting everyone know that you're not bloody working.'

'Boss, will I...?'

'Get the push. Bloody soft aren't you? Piss off and for Christ's sake find some other way of wasting yer bloody time.'

So Smudge pressed on to the ninth floor and found the other two lift attendants waiting there.

'Anyfing doin?' he called.

'Nuffin' much.'

'Surprising i'n'it? Ninth floor's usually seething ov people!' Smudge said.

The indicator board buzzed. All three stepped inside their lifts.

'It's the sixth,' said Softee.

'It's the sixth,' echoed Charlie Byrd

Smudge stood his ground.

'Didn't yer 'ear it, Smudge? Call on the sixth.'

'Yer, just picked 'er up.'

''Er?'

'Yeah.'

'Nice?'

'Quite.'

'Old?'

'Young.'

'Bit of a...'

'Yer that's 'er.'

Charlie stepped back into his lift and the gates clanged shut. Smudge watched the red six disappear from his indicator board, and soon after more numbers started to light up. Charlie was in for a busy time. He wondered how he'd got on with his be-furred lady on the sixth floor. Smudge smiled. It wasn't a bad day.

Then he looked at his watch. Quarter to five. Soon he would have to move down to pick up the home-goers, but there was just time for a smoke first. He turned to Softee, an old man completely bald, with a square face and a weak voice.

'Wanna drag?' Smudge asked.

'Yer.' Softee trudged off as if he were walking on flippers.

'And Softee...' Softee turned round. 'I want time for one too.'

Softee did not reply but moved off towards the Gents. He came back at five o'clock.

'You great fat bastard,' said Smudge.

'What's the matter?' Softee said looking innocently pained.

'What yer bin' smoking? Bloody king size?'

Smudge stepped inside his lift and let his gates crash behind him. He watched the red lights eaten up by Charlie Byrd's progress. Then a red light appeared in his wake and Smudge leaned back on his lever.

'The Girl on the Seventh Floor' stepped into the lift and smiled. She was about the only girl on the seventh floor who ever smiled.

'Ground please.'

'Yeah, it's all ground at this time.'

Red lights were coming and going and Smudge assumed that Softee was back at work.

'Had a nice day?' the girl asked.

Smudge stared.

'Oh... er... yes. Very nice.' He couldn't remember a nice young girl talking to him before.

Before Smudge noticed, the lift had sailed past the ground floor on its way to the basement missing several home-goers en-route. It was always difficult to get back from the basement on this lift. He strained at the lever. Eventually the lift began to move and came to rest at the ground floor.

'Goodnight,' the girl said.

'Good... er sorry about the er... lift, I...' But the girl was gone.

Smudge stood looking down the corridor but she had hurried out of the door. His indicator board was buzzing with red lights. He stepped inside the lift and started towards the eighth floor. He collected passengers. But again he took them to the basement.

Smudge turned on his lift and stepped inside. Charlie had been on since six; it was his week for early stints. Smudge was lucky this week - no early mornings and no lates. He stepped inside the lift and ascended till he reached the seventh floor.

Someone had pressed the button on the ground floor. He pulled the lever backwards, but it wasn't her. How could he expect it to be with so many people in the building?

After the rush he went to the ninth floor to join Charlie and Softee.

'I'm going for a fag,' he said.

'No, you ain't,' said Charlie. 'You go after me.' Smudge waited while Charlie strode towards the Gents.

He heard a buzz on a lower floor.

'There's someone at three,' said Softee.

'No? Yer don't say?'

'They'll get impatient.'

'Let 'em.'

Softee shrugged and stepped inside his lift.

When the red light lit up on the indicator for the seventh, Softee had already passed it. Smudge closed his gate with the lever and, in his eagerness to get to the seventh floor, opened them again. Second time he did it more slowly and the lift rumbled down.

It was the girl. She stepped into the lift and smiled.

'You're always first here,' she said.

He noticed the red skirt she was wearing, and the fish net tights. He noticed too the way her pert breasts pressed against the white wool of her sweater.

'Second please,' she said.

He made an effort of concentration. She would not travel in his lift if he always took her to the wrong floor. When the big figure 3 was half way up the grill, he eased the handle to 'stop'.

She smiled again and he watched her as she disappeared down the corridor. Then he remembered Charlie. He pushed the lever hard forward. The gates flew shut but the lift did not move. He returned the lever to 'stop', moved it forward slowly and the gates shut. Then he jerked the handle out and eased it forward; the lift began to move upwards.

When he reached the ninth Charlie was waiting for him. He knew there would be trouble because an unattended lift switched on meant trouble. Whenever anyone went for a smoke someone had to mind his lift so that he didn't have to switch it off. That would let everyone on every floor know that one of the lifts was out of operation.

He was ready for Charlie when he opened the door.

'Why dyer leave the ninth?'

'There were a call,' said Smudge apprehensively.

'Softee could've picked it up.'

'But 'e weren't near.'

Smudge felt his collar tighten as Charlie's hands gripped him. Then, with a thud, he hit the back of the lift and slithered to the floor. He didn't know what happened after that. All he could hear was a voice saying: 'Get up. Get up.'

Then Charlie's powerful hands pulled him to his feet.

'Stand at the bleedin' door until you feel better,' he said.

Smudge propped himself against the lift door and waited for the dizziness to pass.

'Now go and have a drag.'

Smudge shook his head.

'I said go and have a drag.'

He pulled out a packet of cigarettes and sauntered towards the Gents. Then he locked himself in a cubicle and put the cigarettes back into his pocket. He sat back on the seat and held his head in his hands, sobbing. For ten minutes he stayed like this. Then he went to the washstand and splashed water on his face, towelling himself with the dirty roll towel on the wall.

11

When he got back to the lift Charlie was waiting for him.

'O.K.?' Charlie asked.

'Shutup.'

Charlie did not speak, just watched as Smudge stepped inside his lift and pulled the lever back. There was someone waiting to use the lift on the ground floor. Where had he left the girl? He had forgotten, but both the other lifts had stopped picking up passengers so he went down to collect.

It was the woman in furs. She stepped in without a word. Then, as they rose past the second floor, she said:

'Do I need to tell you it's the sixth floor I want?'

Smudge did not answer.

'You're very quiet young man. You look as if you've been crying.'

Smudge scowled at her and turned to study the floor numbers as they passed the lift door.

'Six,' he said.

The lady in furs got out.

'Wait for me young man. I'll only be two minutes.'

'Silly bleedin' cow,' he muttered, and leaned against the wall.

After a few moments she did return.

'Ground floor, young man,' she said

Smudge set the lift in motion.

'And do you think we could have a less bumpy stop this time? I felt very sick after yesterday's ill-temper on your part.'

Smudge stared and, without thinking, let go of the handle. The lift came to a halt. He stared stupidly at the handle, then an idea dawned in his mind.

'Start the lift up again young man,' said the lady in furs.

Smudge just stared at her. Then he raised his hand to his aching head and he noticed her flinch. He had never before realised the power he had over people. He did not re-start the lift, just stood staring at the woman and watching the colour drain from her face.

'Start the lift, young man,' she said, this time without the ordering tone.

'My husband...'

'Sod yer husband,' said Smudge and lifted his hand again. He liked to watch her flinch. Every time he moved she flinched. By now

12

she was standing in the corner, clutching her firs around her, her face so deadly white that her red lipstick stood out like red paint on a corpse.

'Please start the lift,' she murmured.

'Please start the lift,' he mimicked.

'If you just started the lift now I wouldn't say anything to my husband. I wouldn't say anything to anyone.'

Smudge just stared at her.

'What do you want me to do?' she asked.

'Nuthin',' Smudge said. 'I just like to see yer like you are now.' He pushed the lever backward and then moved his hand hard down. The lift moved. Between the second and first floor he stopped again.

'I don't think you 'ad better tell anyone.'

'No, I won't,' she said quickly.

'Won't do yer no good if you do,' he said, 'I'll just say the lift got stuck and you being the bloody ol' baggage yer are thought I was gonna molest yer. That'll give 'em a laugh!'

She didn't speak, just nodded, and Smudge set the lift in motion again. When he set her down, he turned off his lift and went for a tea break. He never heard from the lady in furs again, but he did hear from Softee that she had started to walk up to the sixth floor. It made Smudge laugh every time he thought about it.

He sat down at a table and pulled out a chocolate biscuit. One of the messengers came to sit on his table. Smudge waited for him to sit down. Then he said: 'I 'ad a bird last night.'

'Had?'

'Yes, she were... Christ she were somethin'.'

'Since when have you had a bird?'

'Since yesterday.'

'What was she like?'

'Like I was tellin' yer. She had smashing legs. And Christ! - her tits. When she took her jumper off, you should have seen what happened.'

'What, they dropped off?'

'No, they never dropped off. They was big, see. Like bloody marrers and bloody big nipples you could hardly get your hand round.'

The messenger stared amusedly at Smudge. Others, grinning, joined their table.

'You ever hear of a bird with bulging knockers showin''er tits to Smudge here?' asked the first messenger.

'No reason why not,' said another, 'some birds'll show their tits to anyone. They 'ave to give 'em a bleedin' airing or they don't grow proper-er.'

Smudge smiled happily and cupped his hand round his mug of tea as if it were a woman's breast.

He chinked his mug back in its saucer and rose from the chair.

'Bloody big they were,' he said as he left the room, 'like bleedin' marrers.'

When Smudge got back to the lift, a red seven glowed on his indicator board. He moved his lift to the seventh floor and his gates crashed open. It was the girl again. She smiled and stepped inside.

'One please,' she said.

'One,' Smudge said as if giving the matter a lot of thought.

The lift began to move downwards. The girl was staring at him.

'You... You're all red round the eyes,' she said.

His hand flew to his face in an effort to hide his eyes. The lift shuddered to a halt. Smudge mumbled apologies and put his hand back on the handle.

'I'm sorry. Did I upset you?' she said.

'No.' He smiled. 'No, I get sore eyes. I 'ave to go to the doctor. He gives me stuff and that but it don't do no good.'

He looked at the girl but did not pull down the lever. For the second time that day his mind dwelt upon his new power. There was no need to move on, and whatever he did there was not much she could do about it.

He watched her breasts heaving as she breathed and her legs as she lifted the hem of the dress to pick off a piece of cotton.

'I like yer dress,' Smudge said.

'Thank you.' She did not seem worried to be stuck between floors with him. But she, he reflected, was different. Again he watched the swell of her breasts and again he resisted the temptation to touch them. Instead he pulled back the lever and the lift moved down to the first floor.

For four or five weeks Smudge took the 'Girl on the Seventh Floor' up and down in his lift. But one day he did not see her at all. The following morning he waited anxiously for a red seven to show on the indicator board. When it did he jumped into his lift while Charlie and Softee stared at each other, surprised at his urgency.

When he opened the lift gates, he saw it was her. She stepped in and smiled.

'One please.'

He moved the lever.

'Ill were yer yesterday?'

She looked up.

'No, day's leave. I was getting things ready.'

'Ready?'

'Yes, I'm leaving tomorrow. I'm moving and I had a lot of jobs to do. You know how it is.'

Smudge nodded and stared at the indicator board.

'I'll be on the seventh at four-thirty if you want to say goodbye,' she said. 'They're letting me go early.'

He smiled and nodded again.

At four-fifteen he waited on the eighth floor ready to drop to the seventh as soon as he saw by the indicator board that she was there. At four-twenty five his indicator buzzed. He was ready to ignore it if it were any other floor but the seventh, but it was the seventh. He pulled back the lever.

But it was not the girl. It was a middle aged woman. She stepped inside and Smudge checked that there was no one else in the corridor. He took the woman to the basement and then stopped for someone on the first: 'Basement,' he said.

'Can't yer walk?' said Smudge.

But the man couldn't walk and he didn't take kindly to the suggestion that he might. As he descended to the basement the red seven on his indicator board lit up. Smudge dropped the man at the basement and pushed the lever forward. But the red seven disappeared. Someone had picked her up. He looked at his watch. It was four thirty. He took his lift to the seventh but there was no one else waiting. He watched lower numbers disappear from his indicator board as the other lift descended. He waited. Smudge heard someone coming.

'Sorry I'm late,' a voice said.

It was the girl! He grinned broadly as she stepped in. He could hear hurrying footsteps down the corridor but he snapped the gates shut and pulled back the lever.

'It's sad leaving,' the girl said.

'Yeah, It's sad I know,' said Smudge.

The girl smiled:

'I'm all ready for the move. I've got a job up there.'

Smudge's hand came off the lever. This time it was not an accident and they were between the fourth and third floors. He looked at her face but she showed no sign of fear. His hand moved towards her, but he could not touch her.

'It won't be the same yer know. Takin' yer up 'n' down so long and that. It don't seem the same knowing - you know - that yer going.'

Still she smiled.

Smudge sadly reached for the lever and pulled it slowly back. They descended to the ground floor in silence, but when they reached it she did not leave the lift but moved towards him. He wondered what she was going to do. She patted his cheek and said:

'You've been so nice. Bye.'

Then, slowly, she walked out of the lift.

'Er... lady,' said Smudge.

'Yes?'

'Bye,' said Smudge.

'Bye.'

The 'Girl on the Seventh Floor' walked slowly away from the lift and down a small flight of steps. He watched her go and stood staring down the corridor long after she had gone out of the door. Then he got back into the lift and swung the lever forward, ignoring the red lights which buzzed angrily on his indicator panel. When he reached the ninth floor he stopped, turned off his lift and stood staring at the wall.

The Chirping Crickets

A selection of rock 'n' roll music blared tinnily from the tannoy and the air was full of the noise of the fair. Mike and I stood by the dodgems appraising the talent. There were no girls worth the quid that a go would cost.

The sun had baked the dusty grass and we were glad of the shade of the dodgem circuit's faring. We watched the cars going round and round; there wasn't even any healthy bumping. But at the moment there was no one worth bumping - girls out for a laugh, giggling at the wheel. Expecting it. Enjoying it. We wandered over to some of the other stands knowing they would come.

But the other attractions held little interest for us. We were interested in the cars. I remembered the track at Rhyl where they had a rogue car. You'd get offered a day of free rides if you could handle it - but you never could. And things were made worse by being the centre of attraction. The other cars came at you as if you had a magnet attached to you and every spin seemed to go on for ever while you fought madly to keep control.

And the previous year's fair at Carshalton. That was funny. I was driving and Mike was passenger - these days we have a bit more cash and could afford a car each with which to harry some hapless female. But then we had just pocket money and we had to select our rides with care.

I spotted a sailor. We didn't normally go for blokes but he was so beautifully positioned that I couldn't resist it. I drove straight at his car, hitting him side on. It was the best place to hit them to put them in a spin. But it also left them in a good position for pursuit if they managed to control it.

And he was good. He swung the wheel and set off in pursuit. I noticed that, as I hit him, he had hit his knee painfully on the side of the car. It showed in his face. Not a pleasant face I imagine at the best of times.

I led him a pretty good dance but when I got to the side of the track there was nowhere else to go. I positioned the car sideways on to the ledge around the track, snug against it. That way it stopped the worst effect of the impact and your aggressor just bounced off.

But as the sailor approached it was obvious that he had taken his foot off the pedal. He was just coasting towards us. I toyed with the idea of making a quick move but realised that, as soon as we moved, he had us at a disadvantage. I just waited to see what he would do.

Then, to my amazement, he leaned out of the car and punched Mike in the face. Mike was too surprised to say anything but the sailor said a lot. It wasn't the sort of language you'd repeat to your Mum.

I started up and accepted all the bumps that came without re-taliating. The biggest irony was when we were shunted from behind and cannoned into a stationary car which was positioned by one of the operators. I think he must have had his foot dangling over the track between the side and the car because I got a real earful. And then Mike rounded on me.

The sailor seemed to have forgotten us; in fact he never came near us again. Obviously recognising our existence was something he preferred not to do.

I stumbled out of the car and walked unsteadily to the rifle range. I looked back and saw Mike. He was sitting on the grass nursing the biggest shiner I had ever seen.

Sailors are transient people and we had never seen him since. As far as I was aware Mike bore no grudges and, after all, if he had been in the driver's seat he would have done precisely the same.

He threw a few darts, in a desultory fashion, which hit the metal rim of the dart board and paid over another quid for some more throws.

'You've done this before haven't you?' muttered the bloke in charge. 'I'm not sure that I want you to have another go - winning all the prizes.'

I wasn't sure whether he was egging Mike on or whether he was being just plain sarky. I decided the former - to mock one's clientele meant a poor financial return at the end of the day. In which case he must have thought Mike was born yesterday, because his darts arm was about as bad as mine.

But then we were only really marking time until the dodgems warmed up. We could see two girls walking slowly towards the cars, wondering whether to go on. Mike threw his dart but he hadn't even been looking at the board. His attention was on the girls.

He looked at me and I nodded. Then he walked away from the darts stand leaving the darts - and a very perplexed stall holder - behind him.

The two hadn't decided to go on the dodgems. They were looking at the other cars in a bored fashion, one tapping her feet to the Buddy Holly record rasping over the tannoy.

I hummed along, singing a few of the words:

'I'm just sittin' here reminiscing, wondering who you've been kissin' baby. Wo-ho-ho-baby.'

The girl nearest glared.

'I like him,' she said pointing at the tannoy as if it had a life of its own.

'Buddy Holly?' I queried.

'Well it ain't Winston Churchill is it?' she replied.

She was chewing. Mike could have her.

I turned my attention to the other girl but she looked away. They were both pretty so I decided mine was the shy one. I didn't think she'd looked away out of repulsion.

More Buddy Holly followed. The saucy one was lucky. I left her to her luck - and Buddy. And possibly Mike.

To her friend I said:

'Do you fancy a go?'

She just looked at me blankly.

'I'll pay for a car. We could share one.'

She smiled. I decided it was quite the most beautiful smile I had seen. She said:

'Thanks - really. But I don't think I'd better.'

I waited for the cars to stop and freed a stationary one from the two alongside.

'Come on,' I said.

The girl smiled. Then stood, looking unhappy. Mike had pushed out a car and the other girl had stepped into it.

'What's your name?' I asked the shy girl.

'Susan.'

'Come on then Susan. Just a ride.'

'I don't think I...'

'They're collecting the money, come on.'

The collector stood between me and the girl. I looked round him to shout.

'Come on Susan - before it's too late.'

The collector put his hand on the car's pole.

'Quid, Romeo. I don't think the lady's coming. Or do you want to book two cars?'

He was being sarky of course but I ignored it. It gave me an idea. 'Susan. Do you want another car? I'll pay for it.'

I paid over two quid but Susan didn't want to.

I cursed under my breath and swung the steering wheel. Mike was careering round with his arm round the other girl. Stupid fool. He deserved to be rammed and I decided to do it for him.

What I didn't see was the other car to my left. I kept Mike to my right and then, just as he turned, I went for him.

It didn't work. Mike saw me coming and turned into me. In time to stop himself spinning and to knock me into the path of the car on my left. Whoever was driving this I don't know, but he didn't miss the opportunity. He got me side on and I nearly lost hold of the steering wheel.

I looked up to see how Susan was taking this but she wasn't looking. Perhaps she couldn't bear to witness my ignominy. Perhaps she was worried lest I was hurt and didn't want to show it. Perhaps she didn't care a tinker's cuss and was waiting for the other girl so she could go home.

I managed to avoid trouble for the rest of the go; then I tried again. I leaned out of the car.

'Please Susan. Just one go. I'll keep out of trouble.'

She smiled. If she didn't like me why did she keep smiling at me? The collector came around again.

'Another go Romeo? Juliet going to risk a battering this time is she?' He turned to where Susan was staring glassily at the hoop-la stand.

'Doesn't look like it does it friend?' he said.

I had to admit it didn't.

'I paid you two quid last time,' I said righteously.

'Very generous I thought that. But one was for the lady.'

'But she didn't...'

'Didn't she? Didn't see meself. Thought she must have done.'

I cursed and dug into my pocket for another pound. He leapt onto the next car as mine started moving.

Then I saw that Mike and the other girl had got off and were collecting Susan on their way God-knew-where.

I took the car to the side cursing the silly sod who tried to ram me back towards the middle.

And I ran headlong into the collector.

'I'm surprised you spend so much money on 'em if you don't really like them.'

He obviously thought this very funny and I could hear him laughing long after I had pushed past him.

I ran from one stand to another and round all the flying, gyrating and pulsating machinery in which people had paid good money to be terrified - or have their stomachs turned over.

And when I found Susan she was with Mike. I couldn't believe it. Mike was a friend.

I don't know where the other girl was - but Mike had obviously made his choice. He spotted me over his shoulder and grinned. I wandered back to the dodgems. Buddy was singing again:

'One lonely night.' It would be. I had misjudged everything. Buddy echoed my thoughts:

'What a foo-ool I've been.'

As the Holly medley burst into *It Doesn't Matter Any More*, I sat on the edge of the dodgem track and watched. Any other time I should have been diving for a car. The little redhead in the green car was being hemmed in on four sides - and she was screaming and laughing all at the same time. The cars stopped. Four hands reached out the money for her next ride.

I walked slowly towards a car, put one hand on the wheel and one on the car's pole. Then I jumped away from the car. Half an hour ago I should have been in that car like a shot but now I didn't care about the little redhead. Or the giggling girls who were climbing into the cars on the far side.

And then two things happened which destroyed my faith in human nature. Firstly I saw the sailor - the sailor! And he had seen me. Obviously memories lingered long with him for he recognised me immediately and pointed towards the car I had just vacated.

I looked at it for a few minutes then shook my head. I had no stomach for the fight. Especially if I won the duel on the track and he resorted to his previous revenge tactics.

The second thing that happened was the appearance of Mike - with Susan of course. His nearness to the sailor made me wonder. Could he possibly have told him I was around - perhaps even suggested that I wanted a return fight?

No I couldn't believe it of Mike. He was my mate.

Then I looked at Susan, smiling happily beside him. And then I could think anything of Mike. No crime was too heinous for him to commit.

I wondered whether the affair with the sailor the previous year had gone deeper than I had thought. It seemed incredible but Mike's behaviour had made the incredible credible.

I kicked the car.

The collector rounded on me.

'You really don't like them do you? Trying to kick the habit now are we?' Again he retired delighted with his own wit.

I pushed my hands deeper into my leather windcheater and made towards the exit. The sun disappeared behind a cloud and Buddy sang softly 'lonesome tears, sad and blue. I've cried lonesome tears for you'. Past the darts stand and the coconut shy I could hear the distant refrain of *Raining In My Heart*. I watched for a few moments while an ardent youth collected a prize at the shy and thrust it into the hands of the girl at his side. The kiss she gave him was long and passionate. I'd heard kissing spread diseases and hoped that this one had.

Then I saw a vision. Susan was standing in front of me. But where was Mike? She smiled - cautiously.

'Mike's been talking.'

'I bet,' I retorted angrily.

'He's been saying you're nice.'

I didn't reply.

'He said all the bravado isn't really you.'

I wondered what bravado she meant. I continued to stare at her and I think it made her feel uncomfortable.

'He's gone on the dodgems with Sally. I don't really like dodgems - I'm sorry.'

My side of the conversation was not doing my reputation for volubility justice. Again I stared stupidly.

'But I do love fireworks,' she said. 'Mike said you love fireworks. Would you take me to the display tonight?'

A shell burst in my head scattering a multitude of electric stars. Giant saxon wheels spun; a flight of a hundred rockets sped skyward, bursting into green, red and blue stars. Comets blazed across the sky, hummer stars and flash Roman candles filled the park with noise.

And the sun reappeared to the distant accompaniment of Buddy Holly as he sang:

'Ready set. Go man go. I've got a girl that I love so.'

Rome Calling Albert Belcher

The sun shone through the wide expanse of glass onto the bowed head of Albert Belcher and it seemed to him that he was back in Rome, or perhaps St Marks Square, serenading his love with a boyish enthusiasm.

But Albert Belcher was not most people's idea of a lover. He was small - dwarfed behind the bulk of the visible index which conveniently hid him from the eagle eyes of Miss Farraday - with a pale, decidedly unhealthy, countenance. It was not enhanced by his use of a green eye shade which was, he professed, necessary for the protection of his eyes but which, most of his colleagues felt, was merely the finishing touch to the image he nurtured of the ex-journalist.

Neither was the image entirely assumed. He had, indeed, worked in the offices of a national daily in Fleet Street and his writing skill was not inconsiderable - as was evidenced by the science fiction novel which he had once produced - uncut - on the insistence of a colleague. And, while he never boasted his skill, which was as apparent as the envy of the redoubtable Miss Farraday, he did parade his association with famous names in the literary world with whom he was apparently in constant touch at his local 'literary' public house.

And it may all have been true. The spy who had been detailed to attend the riverside pub to verify his stories had seen him there and had had pointed out to him a few of the famous people whose company he had claimed to occasionally share. And, if he was not actually in their company on that particular evening, he was not ignored by the hostelry's clientele.

An unexpected extra news item with which the 'spy' was able to regale his colleagues arose when Albert Belcher suddenly fell gracefully backwards from his position at the bar to be quickly revived and returned to the company of his friends.

The reasons for his collapse were obscure. He never mentioned any disability - other than the reluctance of his eyes to stand the sun's full glare - and the few half pints he had consumed were scarcely sufficient to cause his sudden instability.

Albert Belcher was, thankfully, unaware of the witness to his collapse and was able to resume work the following morning without the knowledge that, for the first time since taking the job, he was the talk of the office.

It was a state of affairs which was not to last very long. Despite the veneer - for his colleagues felt it was a veneer - of literary respectability, his journalistic background was felt to be of little interest and, largely because of the sneering invective of the redoubtable Miss Faraday, was beginning to assume the appearance of a carefully constructed myth.

And, in fairness to Albert Belcher, he had never claimed to have done more than work in a newspaper office; it was in the wearing of the editorial eye-shade that his colleagues considered that he was living a lie.

So the stock of Albert Belcher slumped for a time to be temporarily revived at the beginning of the telephone calls from Rome. But it was to be those very calls that would eventually be his undoing.

The first came on the morning at which this narrative commences. Albert Belcher's sun shaded eyes were staring intently at the circulation slips in front of him, with sunny Italy twinkling in his normally fish like eyes and nervous anticipation apparent in his normally calm movements.

He pulled a drawer of the visible index towards him, made various markings on a card, and withdrew a slip from the card's holder. He transcribed a circulation list from the slip onto the back of a periodical and placed it in his out tray for collection.

It was Miss Farraday's belief that one in four of the periodicals which left his desk had at least one error. She had caught him three times in the act of transcribing a list from a different periodical and, more than once, in making errors in the names he was copying. To Miss Farraday, this represented gross negligence and led to her claim - which must have been a wild guess - that exactly twenty five per cent of his work was defective.

However it is to the middle managers - the Miss Farradays of this world - that authority listens and, short of performing the impossible task of examining every piece of work that left his desk, those in authority were unable to do other than accept her assessment.

But, if Miss Farraday were to have stood by his desk on the morning in question - to her subsequent great regret she was attending a meeting - she would have had plenty of material for an immediate report on the inaccuracy of Albert Belcher's work. She might have been able to achieve her desired objective of his removal from her office.

For Albert Belcher was unquestionably apprehensive. He was heard to hum - he was usually given to singing in a loud, irritating - but not untuneful – baritone, but rarely hummed. He tapped his pen while scanning the circulation lists and when the telephone rang - as it frequently did - he dropped whatever was in his hands in an effort to grasp the 'phone before his colleague on the other side of his desk had a chance to do so.

So far Albert Belcher had merely received double the normal quota of complaints - for he politely and humbly apologised for the errors of his colleagues without first assessing - as was the usual practice - the member of staff to whom the complainant should have been directed.

If nervous Albert Belcher was clearly in a good mood. He smiled at old Mrs Young - the ironically named decrepit to whom smiles were rarely directed - and accepted cheerfully the violent invective of Gimbu, the Nigerian agency typist to whom Belcher - strangely - represented the worst of colonial oppression.

Good humour and acceptance of the inevitable abuse were in his nature but such encounters with Miss Young and Gimbu had rarely been met, even by Belcher, with such humility and forbearance.

But he was becoming more casual in his answering of the telephone. His hopes had been dashed too many times for his boyish expectation to remain undiminished.

And it was of course when he was at his most blasé that the call came through.

The office was unprepared, though used to Albert Belcher's deep sonorous voice, for the mightily loud love making that ensued.

'Dar-ling,' he barked. 'You have, you have. How splendid. How perfectly splendid, oh! but I am longing to see you again... yes it is beautiful in London - very hot, and how is it in Rome...? Splendid, splendid... I have been thinking of no one but you.'

Until this point the unheard second party to the conversation had clearly been mouthing appropriate questions but now began to take upon herself a greater share of the exchange. His replies became monosyllabic - even disintegrated into grunts as his forehead glistened and his eyes held in them the look of a man deeply - deeply in love.

The conversation which lasted for perhaps fifteen minutes was the first of many. The staff began to expect them - coming as they did at about the same time every other day.

And after that first call Belcher's colleagues sank rather more deeply into their work than was usual - vaguely embarrassed and unwilling to show what was a perfectly natural curiosity.

For a few moments Albert Belcher contented himself with a snatch from an Italian opera but this could satisfy his bursting heart only momentarily. He scanned the apparently industrious down-bent heads of his colleagues hoping for a raised eye - a glimmer of curiosity. But none came.

He lifted a pile of periodicals and then put them down. With such a joy upon him displaying such an obvious desire to break the restricting bounds of his heart, he could concentrate on no such mundanities. And with Miss Farraday attending her meeting, his coast was clear for a quick - a very quick - conversation with one of his colleagues.

He chose as the recipient for such valued information the only person - a boy scarcely out of his teens named Smith - who had previously shown any interest in him as a person rather than a curiosity. He recalled that it was Smith who had asked to read his book and had shown by his knowledge of it that he had actually read it; actually negotiated with extreme difficulty the uncut pages without affecting its pristine condition.

Belcher approached him - stopped as if it had been his original intention to pass - exclaimed 'Mamma Mia' as if it was an instinctive exclamation which he had been unable to control, and sighed deeply shaking his head and smiling as if at the wonder of life.

His colleague looked up nervously, smiled, and transferred the pen with which he had been working from his hand to his mouth as if, thereby, he could more easily facilitate his reception of the unburdening of Belcher's soul.

But before the action was complete, Belcher had already embarked upon an explanation of the telephone conversation.

'That was Maria,' he said proudly as if the statement were sufficient to explain his enthusiasm.

'Maria?'

'We,' Belcher grinned, 'we have an understanding.'

Smith smiled as if the statement explained much.

'She is your...?'

'Yes, yes,' nodded Belcher madly. 'Yes indeed' (this with a happy sigh).

Smith waited for more but it was unforthcoming. It seemed that the revelation of the lady's identity and the - rather cryptic - nature of their relationship were sufficient to satisfy the speaker's need to impart some information.

And, indeed, the ardour of that relationship was demonstrably evident each time the telephone rang and the voice of Albert Belcher boomed his now customary introductory 'Dar-ling'.

The rest of the staff were able to glean little pieces of further information both from Albert's end of the conversation and his answers to Smith's polite enquiries after the lady's health.

'Ah, she is well, my Maria,' Belcher would begin, his eyes raised to the ceiling as if she were about to appear in answer to his fervent wishes. But the conversation always assumed a more earthly nature and Belcher would reveal that she had 'been to Naples' or that she would not be 'phoning because she was 'visiting the States'.

It seemed inevitable that this much travelled lady would eventually arrive in London and so it transpired but, before the trip was arranged, the interest in the mysterious lady had waned. Smith kept up his polite enquiries; the two middle aged ladies asked after her, but the novelty of the unromantic Albert Belcher having a romantic lover was an office topic for only as long as it took another to arise.

Miss Young feigned a lack of interest, while talking loudly in Albert's hearing about the wickedness of using the telephone at the most expensive time of the day. Belcher subsequently explained that Maria had the use of her office telephone and that her calls cost her nothing, but this incensed her further into delivering a diatribe about people who used public funds as if they were their own.

These remarks Albert Belcher chose not to hear, treating Miss Young with his usual civility and retaining his boyish enthusiasm for 'his love in sunny Roma'.

Gimbu, too, was ignored but he was ignored by most of the staff - as presumably he expected to be. For if his vitriolic attacks on everyone and everything were to be seriously considered they would long before have earned him an accusation of slander or a broken head.

To Gimbu, Maria was naturally a fascist, and her relationship with Belcher was clearly further evidence of either infantile regard or approaching senility. For a middle aged man to be happy was an anathema to Gimbu and, until the arrival of an Indian gentleman whose quiet and kindly nature suggested that he could be more easily hurt than the resilient Belcher, Maria was the favourite subject of his barbs of vicious wit.

But largely it was disinterest rather than spite that was directed towards Albert and his lady – until, that is, the looked for meeting in London was announced.

Maria came to London in the spring and, for a time at least, the telephone calls did not have to be born.

Albert Belcher took two weeks' leave and Smith and the middle aged ladies at least looked for his return with a certain amount of curiosity.

And when Albert Belcher did return it was with a fat wadge of photographs which his three curious colleagues pounced upon with great interest, while even Miss Farraday and Miss Young made quite unnecessary trips to the stationery cupboard to encompass en route the photograph strewn Belcher desk.

And it was with some surprise that these curious eyes discerned a plump homely looking dark haired lady of not unattractive features - the possessor of a winning smile which was frequently directed towards the small grinning figure at her side.

But again the enthusiasm waned. Maria returned to Rome and the routine of regular 'phone calls resumed. Even the amenable Smith confessed to some irritation at the monotony of that boomed 'Dar-ling' which some other members of staff had begun to dread.

And it was only three weeks after their resumption that Miss Farraday had 'words' about them. Albert nodded in agreement that they took up too much of his time, agreed readily that their length should be curtailed and, for a week, made some excuse for reducing their length to the original fifteen minutes.

This was not enough for Miss Farraday. One a week was sufficient - an arrangement with which again Belcher concurred. And for a while the calls were less frequent although not as infrequent as promised. However Belcher obviously had not the heart to forbid the calls that meant so much to him and they began to return to their original duration and frequency.

Belcher explained that Maria could not have afforded to make the calls in her own time and revealed to Smith only that his lady had had certain troubles of her own as a result of her employers' understandable reluctance to finance her love life.

To Smith's suggestion that they should write, Albert smiled sadly and confessed that he had not enough Italian - an admission which came as some surprise to his colleagues who, used to his use of short utterances in that language, had assumed that he was proficient in its use.

Smith secretly felt that, if his love was great enough, Belcher would learn to write Italian or his lady, clearly able to express herself adequately in English over the telephone, should reach a standard of written English sufficient to express her feelings in letters to him.

As a letter writer himself, Smith was unable to understand that Belcher's romance could not flourish without the very necessary spur of the sound of the loved one's voice, heard frequently over the wires. He was too callow, also, to accept that Maria could not throw up her job and fly to Albert Belcher's side, there to remain.

There were others who could not understand that the telephone calls were essential to Belcher's romance - perhaps that a public avowal, even, was necessary to its furtherance. And to be fair Miss Farraday was one of these.

There was a lot that Miss Farraday did not know. She was not aware that Maria's globe-trotting was on official business and that her Italian employers paid a wage which - to that lady - justified her abuse of the telephone time for which they paid.

And if Miss Farraday did not understand Albert Belcher, she was in the majority and it came as no surprise to the other employees who constituted that majority when that august lady cried 'Enough' and applied for a transfer 'to further Albert Belcher's career'.

Belcher's new job did not involve the use of a telephone and, while he was to be seen crossing the square to the public call box, it was apparent that his calls were not successful in locating the lady whose wandering commission had necessitated her making of the calls in the first place.

Even these hopeful but obviously fruitless attempts at contact were eventually halted by a new boss specially selected to control Belcher's propensity for 'time wasting'.

Smith had passed Belcher once in the corridor and received the surprising information that Maria's flat did not contain a telephone, but no other news had been vouchsafed relating to that lady. Belcher's new colleagues did not see any further photographs of Maria and his cheerful contentment and boyish enthusiasm waned. In fact he became a positive depressant on the office atmosphere and it was considered that another move was necessary to ensure the continued development of his career.

And this move entailed a change of building to the east block from which no news of Belcher came and, starved of information from the office's eastern outpost, his old colleagues assumed him to have sought a post with a new employer.

And the new figure behind the visible index became a part of the office furniture - a colourless part perhaps but not one to stir the emotions. It was some time before the staff in that room began to reflect that Albert Belcher had been 'quite a character' and began to miss his bellowing laughter and the sunny hint of Mediterranean romance which he had brought (in retrospect) to the office.

Waiting

Outside the shelter misty rain fell. Through the streaming side windows of the shelter, the dark walls of the Lodge were barely visible. He sat on the seat, his hair wet and the rain running in rivulets down his face and onto his coat.

He looked at the girl in the corner as she peered nervously into her shopping bag and guessed that the bag was empty, serving only as a refuge from the eyes of a stranger. Her hair was dry; she must have been sitting there for at least an hour.

The rain showed no sign of abating and the occupants of the shelter continued to keep the length of seating between them and their thoughts to themselves. Finally he spoke:

'Rotten weather.'

She glanced up at him, her eyes damp, and looked out of the shelter. It was as if she had noticed the rain for the first time.

'It was fine,' she said.

'This morning it was fine. It has been raining for an hour.'

She nodded. They both stared out at the rain. Slowly, under their gaze, the mist shrank back into the distance and hidden landmarks revealed themselves.

'The avenue!' she said. 'You can see the avenue again.'

She continued to stare at the two parallel rows of Lombardy poplars which formed an avenue from the park gates, and he studied the premature marks of age on her young face. The shopping basket lay forgotten on the seat beside her and her tired eyes strained further into the mist as the park was undressed by the sun.

'The avenue is the first thing I remember about the park,' she said. 'My mother would bring me here and I would hide behind the poplars and wait until she came and found me. Then I would run off and she would return to her seat while I hid again. Oh! The patience she had.'

For a moment the girl stopped to watch the sun sail into a dense patch of cloud, casting a pale light on the grass.

'Then she died. My father took me to Scotland but I insisted on coming back with him for the funeral. I wish I hadn't come back - not for the funeral. All I remember is the black sky and the flapping white coat of the priest and the rain forming in pools on the coffin. I didn't think of my mother in there; it was only when we came back to the house and she didn't come out to take my coat or rub my hands that I realised I would never see her again. And there were so many people, eating, drinking and even laughing; I didn't realise then that a funeral buffet was a public statement that life must go on. Then I could only think of my mother - sipping tea in the summer bay with the sun shining on her grey hair...'

The girl stopped, and looked to the end of the shelter where the man was staring at her thoughtfully.

'I am sorry, I didn't mean to...'

He began to move towards her.

'No, she said. 'Please don't.'

He had reached the middle of the shelter. He nodded understandingly and sat again.

It was now barely raining. The mist was sitting on Midsummer Hill beyond the park gates and people were emerging from shelters and doorways to brave the last of the rain. She shook her head as if shaking off a bad dream and ran her hand through her hair.

'Did you go to Scotland?'

She looked at him, startled. 'Scotland?'

'You said your father wanted to settle in Scotland.'

'Oh, I went there with him after the funeral. But I came back.'

She paused and said: 'I think the rain has stopped.'

'Not quite. It's drizzling. You can see it on the windows. What made you come back - was it the avenue?'

Mention of the avenue turned her attention back towards the poplars. The evocative scent of a park after rain hung on the air and the sweet smell of the poplars drifted to them on the breeze.

'I came back to London, but I didn't settle. I rented a couple of rooms and shared a kitchen. Then I came back here. Merrick helped me buy a small house overlooking the park and he moved into it when he managed to sell his own. I came out and walked along the avenue every morning, and I began to notice that a man would walk some way behind me. Once I caught him looking at me, but he looked down as if he hadn't really meant to. I suppose I felt the need to belong to someone as I had belonged to my mother - that was why I married Merrick.'

She looked towards the church where, three years before, she had passed her mother's tombstone as a bride.

'Merrick wanted to move away but I needed the avenue almost as much as I needed him. Perhaps more. I suppose it was selfish. In everything else I would let him have his way but I would not leave the avenue.'

Tears started in her eyes. She picked up the shopping basket and swung it absently in her hand.

'I never want to leave the avenue.'

'And he wants you to?'

'He?'

'Merrick.'

'Merrick left exactly a year after I'd married him. He was an impatient man - he had to keep moving. I often think of him - how he used to be so tender, how he bought me a house overlooking the park. I remembered a poem I had read and wondered "where love went when it was not broken".'

'And you stayed?'

'Of course.'

She looked up at the sky.

'The rain,' she said, 'It's stopped. I really must go.'

'What happened after that - when you were alone?'

She drew a handkerchief from her handbag and dabbed the corners of her eyes. She said as if voicing a thought:

'I thought about the man who'd waited.'

'Waited?'

'The man who'd followed me in my early walks.'

'Yes I know.'

'I didn't say. But I'd seen him often afterwards- walking up my avenue. At first I was afraid of him; then I started to watch him more closely. I don't know how I realised but I did - he was waiting for me. He was wasting his life.'

'Not wasting...'

'Sometimes I saw his face. It was so patient, so kind. But he only waited. After Merrick left, I began to watch for him. I'd spent most of my time at the window. He always walked down the avenue and always looked up at the house.'

'But you never gave a sign.'

'No, I never showed that I noticed him. Merrick came to see me and bring me money. He did not want a divorce - I don't know why. I think he hoped that one day I would go to him and ask him to take me back. It seemed that everyone was waiting - I did too.

'I had only taken one major decision in my life - to marry Merrick - and that had been the wrong one. But we were all getting older. I'm twenty eight now; it seems my youth has been wasted in waiting.

'And the man was waiting. Every morning and evening he walked down the avenue - still waiting.

'I did little things to fill the time. I started to crochet toys. I made small teddy bears, but they looked at me with such sad pitiful faces, it was as if I was giving them unhappiness by making them.'

'And the man waited?'

'Yes. You know. You know he waited.'

'Didn't you ever wonder about him?'

'I often did. I asked myself questions and answered them. I felt sure my answers were right but I didn't dare to test them. If he was other than I thought him...'

'What did you think him?'

She looked at him pitifully, begging not to answer the question but his eyes were turned to the wet grass and he did not see her look.

'I thought him a patient, kind man.'

'You must have thought more than that.'

'I did make some enquiries.'

He continued to stare at the grass as if uncertain of himself.

'I made some enquiries,' she said, 'of my aunt. I did not like her and couldn't really accept any judgement she made but she had told me she had seen him on his walks. So I asked her.'

At last he looked up.

'She couldn't tell me much. She knew he had worked locally and that he had been unpopular. He was lethargic, morose. It didn't fit in with my picture of him.

'Neither could I believe it when she said that he had committed a crime, k... killed...'

She could not repeat the word, but looked out into the park. She picked up the shopping basket.

'I must go. I have to prepare lunch.'

'How could he have killed? He would not have been walking the park. They do not allow murderers to walk freely.'

She stood.

'No, it was silly. I could see that. But...' She hesitated.

'But what?'

'But it made me more determined than ever that my illusion should not be shattered. I had memories of my mother - full of benevolence and thankfulness. And of my father too. He had died just after Merrick left. I had never reached the stage with either of them where adult minds conflict and, just as I would not make decisions to change my life, I would not have my past changed either. I liked to think of the man waiting, walking - even while I waited. I did not want to repeat my experience with Merrick. I... oh, I would have been happier to die.'

She looked at him, still seated, and noticed that he made no effort to follow her. She turned, thought for a moment, and then sat down again on the shelter seat.

The sun had broken through the cloud and the sky was rapidly clearing, while the tall dark poplars of the avenue cast their slanting shadows across the park shelter to the Lodge beyond.

'I still think he is kind,' she continued. 'I would hold to my beliefs whatever else I might hear about him. As you say criminals are locked up and people talk so foolishly - they are so unthinking. Why else would he wait than because he loved me?'

He moved closer and put a protecting hand around her.

'Do you believe that he loved you and that is why he waited?'

'Oh, yes. Yes.' She smiled. And she continued to smile as his hand drew the blade across her throat and dropped it in a pool of blood at her feet.

In For a Penny

'Never get rid of 'em if they don't try.'

'I'm sure they're trying Mrs Webb. I mean Penny, she's trying all over the place 'cept where she'll be welcomed.'

'Well that's what I mean ain't it? She must go after these boys who come down of a weekend...'

'Looking for trouble and girls,' said Archie. 'Yes Mrs Webb, I will grant you she don't look in the right places, but mark my word she looks hard enough.'

Mrs Webb swept a dishcloth over the counter of the bar and Archie removed his beer before it became a victim of her cleaning.

'What about you f'rinstance?' said Mrs Webb.

Archie looked startled. He imagined that Mrs Webb had long known of his liking for Penny.

'What about me Mrs Webb?'

'Well you're a nice young chap' (she said it as if it had just occurred to her).

'A nice steady job in the bank. Pass'bly good lookin'. Why don't you have a bash?'

'But Mrs Webb, I've been trying for years but Penny just won't look at me.'

'Won't look at yer? What yer mean won't look at yer? I seen her lookin' at yer from behind the bar.'

'You have Mrs Webb? When did she look at me?' said Archie with interest.

'Oh, times. And I'll tell yer somefin' Archie Pullman.'

Archie looked at her intently.

'She's lookin' at yer now.'

Archie's head bent lower towards the counter and he whispered: 'Where is she Mrs Webb? Tell me where she is.'

Then a girl of about seventeen walked jauntily past them swinging a yellow bag. Archie caught sight of her blonde hair, her tight cotton dress and her bare legs as she passed through the bar door.

'Hi! Mum,' she called and the door slammed behind her.

'There!' said Mrs Webb in a tone of disgust, 'yer didn't even try.'

'But Mrs Webb, you don't understand.'

'Don't understand my arse. Bloody kids think sex were invented yesterdee. D'yer know the ol' man took one look at me legs in some public bar an' he proposed to me 'fore he'd seen me face.'

Archie sat back on a bar stool. He wondered if Mr Webb had regretted his impulsive proposal once he had seen his future wife's face. He wondered too whether such a proposal would cut much ice with Penny and decided it would not. For a few moments he sat sipping his beer, then Mrs Webb patted the top of his head and came round the bar to sit beside him.

'It ain't allers so easy I know, Archie; some men ain't so impulsive as 'Arold an' there's times as I wish I 'adn't been so impulsive in replyin'. But yer know Penny ain't the only fish in the pond. What about Sue?'

Sue was Penny's younger sister by a matter of hours. Archie did not bother to tell Mrs Webb that Sue would have done as well as Penny, but, if anything, she had shown even less interest in him than her sister.

'Or is it that Fiona you really get on with?' continued Mrs Webb sadly.

Fiona had been Archie's childhood friend until they had left school when Fiona's hankering for a more mature relationship had caused him considerable embarrassment.

'No, Mrs Webb, I don't get on with Fiona but she gets on with me.'

'How debasin'!' stormed Mrs Webb, 'ta throw yerself at a man as doesn't give free ha'pence for yer.'

'I didn't say that Mrs Webb. I'd give more 'n that for her. It's just that she's so ugly she can't throw herself at anyone else.'

'But Archie yer've got too low 'n 'pinion of yerself. You don't have to throw yerself away.'

'I don't intend to throw myself away Mrs Webb, I just been friends with her a long time and it don't seem right to just cast her aside.'

'But that don't signify, Archie. Think of my Sue and what a

warm plump little body she's got. Just think on that,' she said kindly.

But Archie had thought of that and had no intention of 'snuggling down' with Fiona Richards.

'She's like a rat,' Archie said.

'Sue?'

'Fiona. Kissing her is like kissing a pin cushion. You get little prickles in your face.'

Mrs Webb shook her head sadly. Then an idea occurred to her.

'Archie!' she said suddenly.

Archie looked up.

'Have yer thought of somethin' I've thought of?'

Archie wondered what Mrs Webb had thought of.

'Victoria!'

'Victoria?' said Archie 'But Victoria's only sixteen!'

'All the better. Yer lay yer claim earlier and yer get the goods before others start 'avin' the same ideas, and...' Mrs Webb leaned forward and lowered her voice to a confidential tone... 'I bin lookin' at our Victoria lately. I bin goin' in the bathroom an' seein' for myself. An' Victoria's slimmer 'n Penny and Sue but I swear she's got better features.'

Archie wondered what Mrs Webb meant by features and, as it would not be necessary to go into the bathroom to study her daughter's face, he decided she referred to the swelling breasts that he, too, had not been unaware of. Mrs Webb was a strange mixture, he thought, of frankness and prudery.

He drained the last dregs of his beer with the air of someone making a decision. He then clanked his glass down on the counter and stood up.

'Victoria it is then,' he said.

Mrs Webb looked pleased. 'Right then, tonight she will be serving in the bar.'

'How do you know?'

'Because I will tell 'er she'll be serving in the bar.'

'Does she do everything you tell her?'

'Not everything, and don't think I'm makin' yer job easier 'n I've already made it. I'm testin' yer now. If yer don't make Victoria yer don't make any of my daughters.'

The relationship had returned to its old footing. She was no longer a motherly figure, she was the publican's wife whose duty to her daughters outweighed other considerations.

That night Archie walked into the crowded bar and waited until Victoria had finished serving a group of Half of Bitters. He had ample time to study her as he did so. Mrs Webb had been right: She was slimmer than her sisters and yet her pert breasts pressed hard against her white sweater. He traced the outline of her nipples on the wool and was pleased that there was nothing but Victoria making that bulge. Her hair was as blonde as her sisters' and her face, he thought, prettier. But his thoughts on the relative beauty of Mrs Webb's daughters changed with every week. He took a few coins from his pocket and watched her as she made her way across the bar towards him. He could feel his hand shaking and his voice when he spoke sounded far away and unreal.

'Pint of mild,' he said weakly, then with more conviction, 'No, a scotch - a double, I'll have a double scotch please.'

She stared at him blankly.

'What do you want? Mild or scotch?'

'Scotch please. Strong as you can make it.'

'It doesn't come any stronger - only weaker,' said Victoria and laughed.

'Yes of course, er... yes,' finished Archie lamely.

Victoria pressed the rim of a whisky glass against an optic.

'Anything with it?' said Victoria.

Archie will never be able to explain what came over him at that moment. His mouth opened and words poured out which he had never dared to think, much less say. Whatever the reason Archie put his hand over hers and said:

'Yes. I would like you with it. I would like you to come over the counter and I'd like you to come into my bed and...'

His protestations came to an abrupt end when he realised that people in the bar were turning round to stare at him. Then with a final burst of defiance he held her hand in his and said:

'And I'd like to marry you. I really would.'

Victoria made no attempt to withdraw her hand. Her eyes were wide and her face showed utter amazement. It was some time before anyone spoke, and Archie's confidence rose with the obvious effect he had had on his audience.

'Perhaps you would like to step outside a moment, Miss Webb,' he said. 'Atmosphere's a bit stuffy in here.'

Victoria allowed herself to be led by the hand out of the bar and into the street. Archie was still talking.

'Wouldn't be a very fancy wedding of course. Close family, friends.'

Victoria recovered herself sufficiently to speak.

'But Archie!'

'Don't "but Archie" me. Just tell me yes. That's all I want to hear.'

'But Archie. It's so sudden. I mean, I never guessed you...'

'Adored you. Have done for years. Absolutely adored you. Now, can I have your answer?'

'But Archie I... Well. It's very nice I'm sure feeling like that, but it's all a bit sudden. Can I tell you tomorrow night?'

'Alright, but don't forget, the answer must be yes.'

Archie kissed her roughly on the mouth and then started to walk away. Then Victoria shouted: 'Archie!'

He turned round.

'What about your drink Archie?'

'Drink it yourself.' he shouted.

When Archie called at the pub the following evening much of his false courage had drained away. What is more, he thought as soon as he saw Victoria, her self-possession had returned.

Mrs Webb answered the door and ushered him through the bar and up the stairs to a large living room.

'Yerve made an 'it wiv her alright,' she said. 'Just keep like yer was last night an' she'll be eatin' out of yer 'and.'

She disappeared and Archie waited.

He waited for fifteen minutes, enough time to realise that Victoria was using a very successful method by which to meet him on equal terms and destroy the advantage of the night before. Then she came in. The very sight of her was enough to take away Archie's breath. She was dressed in a white frilled shirt and a tight fitting blue skirt which barely covered her buttocks. She sat regally on the settee and motioned Archie to sit beside her.

'Have you got my answer?' Archie asked.

'Well, I have my answer, but it may not be yours,' said Victoria coolly.

'What is it then?'

'Well I'll tell you,' she said smoothing her hands down the side of her skirt, 'but first I wanted to thank you for the whisky.'

'Never mind the whisky, what's your answer?'

'Well it's rather difficult to put into words.'

'It's quite easy,' said Archie angrily. 'Y.E.S. - yes. That's all you have to say.'

'Or N.O. - no.'

'Or that I suppose. Well, what is it?'

'Well it's not as simple as that because you see it's about half way between yes and no.'

Archie sat back on the settee. Victoria, seeing he was not going to press for an answer, went on:

'If it is going to be yes, there will be something you must do to make it yes.'

Archie had considered something like this.

'I have no money,' he said.

'Nor have I. I don't want money.' Then her calculating air disappeared and she leaned over him, a sixteen year old schoolgirl again.

'I want you to do a dare.'

'A dare?'

'Yes, I want you to do something mad and wicked.'

Archie looked at her in amazement.

'Mad and wicked?'

'Yes! Like writing "knickers" all over the church steeple.'

Archie thought for a moment.

'Alright. If you'll promise to be my wife I'll do something more wicked than daubing "knickers" on the church steeple.'

The look of adulation which he had seen on her face the night before returned:

'Oh, how I misjudged you Archie dear.'

Then she flounced out of the room and left Archie wondering what he could do which was sufficiently wicked to satisfy Victoria's demands.

Then he remembered Fiona. He rushed out of the bar, past an astonished Mrs Webb and towards the large white mansion where Fiona had lived for the past twenty four years.

At four o'clock in the afternoon, Victoria received a note which requested her attendance for an entertainment outside the town hall. When she got there she found that a crowd of people had massed themselves outside the building and were gazing up at the roof where a young man was standing on the guttering dressed only in a loin cloth. An act began on her arrival as if it had been the artiste's cue. Archie Pullman, for it was of course he, began to juggle balls, perform hands stands and cartwheels and finally suspended himself from the guttering and moved his body from side to side in a manner which stilled the amazed babble of the crowd below.

At six o'clock on the same day, Archie presented himself at the pub and Victoria's welcome could not hide an element of worship.

'The answer is yes, Archie, oh yes, yes, yes.'

Archie looked at her and smiled.

'Yes. Of course you realised that the outcome of this arrangement was binding on you, but not on me.'

Victoria gripped his arm.

'Yes. I know that, but you must take me now.'

Archie removed her hand and sat down.

'Unfortunately that is not possible.'

'Not possible?'

'No, you see, I had to get permission to go up on that roof - it was the town hall.'

'You don't mean they let you?'

'Yes. Fiona is the mayor's daughter and she arranged it for me. But she had one condition.'

'Not that you...'

'Marry her. Yes that was it I'm afraid.'

'But Archie. Oh, I wish I'd never asked. I wish I'd accepted.'

'So does Penny,' Archie said.

'Penny?'

'Yes, I just met her in the bar. She told me how much more mature she was than you. In fact she offered herself to me.'

'I'll...'

'You'll do nothing. That is if you want to retain my good opinion of you.'

Archie had noticed how Victoria's breasts were seeking to make an appearance.

As she moved her shoulders back, her shirt gave up the unequal struggle and Archie was treated to the sight of a glorious expanse of nipple. He took hold of the shirt's collar and pulled the shirt out of Victoria's waist band.

'You will marry me won't you, Archie?' Victoria asked.

'I'm not at all sure that I can do that,' Archie replied, taking both her breasts in his hands and feeling the nipples ripen in his hand, 'I'm not sure about that at all.'

When Archie returned to his bed sitter, he found Sue waiting for him on the step. He unlocked the door and motioned her to go through.

As soon as Sue was in his room she began to undo the top buttons of her cotton dress.

'Warm isn't it?' said Archie.

Sue looked at him but continued to undo her dress. She let it fall to the ground. She was wearing no underclothing. He sat on the bed and studied her naked body, illuminated as it was by shafts of evening sunlight through the window. The main road traffic rattled by, and Archie began to unzip his flies with the air of one to whom this sort of thing was becoming a daily routine.

And for weeks Sue, Penny and Victoria vied with each other for the favour of his company, and Fiona lovingly supplied him with money and arranged for his name to be put high on the council housing list.

For Archie the weeks passed pleasantly, but he always managed to avoid giving direct answers to direct questions. He was taking much more to staying with Fiona. One night she asked him:

'Archie, are you going to marry me?'

Archie breathed deeply.

'I'm not at all sure that I can do that,' he said. 'I'm not sure about that at all.'

The House of Delights

I couldn't believe my luck; it was still there. And the sun still cast a pattern of net curtains on its ornate face. So the clock still ticked its regular beat!

How strange it should be still moving on, telling a time today when it reminded me of a time so long ago.

The breeze took the curtain and flapped it against the open French window. Lazy summers! Impossible to think that time moves on so quickly.

A little boy appeared; he peeped in shyly at first but acquired a little more courage and pushed open the French window a little wider and stepped inside. He looked around; just as I had, but to him everything was new. I can never remember this room being new to me - it was just always there.

He stepped in timidly and found the sweets on the table. He listened for noises in the kitchen. I found myself listening too. We heard them at the same time. To him they were a sign that his aunt and mother were engrossed in conversation; to me... well, no matter - to me they were just memories.

The boy stepped forward and picked up the basket of sweets, unwrapping one and putting three in his pocket. The pleasure showed on his face as he bit through the outer casing into the sherbet filling. And I just sat there. I found I could not talk to him, nor could I draw his attention to my presence. So I just watched him as he went to the book case. The books were too high for him to reach but he did not wish to touch them. I watched his mouth wording the titles which appeared on the spines.

His sweet was now finished and his attention drawn by another delight. Yes, delight - this was a house of delights. It stood in the corner by the window - an upright box on four legs with sweeping curved wood at the edges. He fingered the handle at the side, considered, and released it, realising this was something about which he did not know enough.

Now the conversation in the kitchen sounded louder. Just as it had pleased him to hear its intensity not a few minutes before, now it annoyed him. Grown ups seemed to have so much patience; for little boys like him things must be done quickly while the magic lasted.

He stared at the box, at the handle, at the bow legs which supported the box. And he popped another sweet into his mouth to fill in the time. Soon his aunt would come in. His aunt would tell him what it was.

He could see his uncle in the garden, kneeling by a bed of roses. The garden was full; he had never seen a garden so full of flowers. The sun shone down. And two deck chairs stood on the lawn.

He wished this day would last for ever. He remembered the section of garden just out of view where large plants rambled behind trellis fencing and where an ornate well tempted the traveller. But his mind was not completely on the end of the garden, nor on the well, nor the flowers, nor his uncle carefully weeding the rose bed. His mind was on the ornate box and its handle, just asking to be turned.

And then his aunt came in. She came in carrying a table cloth under one arm and some plates in the other hand. She smiled at him and expressed mock disapproval at the bulge in his cheek. It would spoil his dinner. And then she noticed his glance. The old gramophone! Why it hasn't been played for years. Oh! It was bought for Sheila when she was a little girl.

Sheila was his aunt's daughter. The boy felt jealous that the gramophone had been bought for someone else. He wished it had been bought for him. But it kept its fascination. His aunt lay the table; then she looked again at the little boy. He looked crestfallen and she could not disappoint him. She had never disappointed him yet. Sometimes when his mother said no, his aunt said yes. She moved over to where he was standing and lifted his hand to the handle.

Yes! He could turn it. He pushed hard down and leant back to bring the handle up again. And when it was fully wound he pushed on it but, no it would break he was told, so he watched as his aunt lifted the lid.

Inside was a large metal implement which swung round onto a green felted turntable. A record! We must have a record. The boy watched as his aunt pulled the lower drawer towards her. Inside were the records, bigger than the gramophone records he had seen. Each must be clean. Every time you play one it must be cleaned.

The boy stared. Every time you play one! Did that mean...?

Some hours passed. Dinner was cleared away. The little boy sat in an enormous padded armchair and let his legs dangle down. His mother had gone to do a little shopping and his uncle was back in the garden. A shadow came over the room and cooler air blew through the French windows. Spots of rain appeared on the windows but his uncle worked on unperturbed.

Then his aunt went to the cupboard. That cupboard contained all sorts of mysteries. And there were the buttons, some of them peculiar shapes; the square box for sweets which you could see through; the nuts and the dates and... and the photographs. The boy watched to see what his aunt would bring. It was the photographs! She brought them to the settee and he leapt out of his chair to go and sit beside her. He had seen the photographs so many times but he never tired of looking at them: pictures of his mother; he thought how beautiful she was; and of his aunt when she was young with uncle and the little girl, Sheila. And Little Grandpa. Mischievous Little Grandpa. Little Grandpa who used to tell him tales he had never forgotten.

His aunt could remember such fascinating things about his Grandpa; about everybody. He leant nearer to his aunt to get a better look at the photographs and, by the time the album was closed, the rain had stopped.

He wondered whether he would go down to the end of the garden or whether he would just sit and wait for tea. It was fish - sole. There was nothing like sole and he knew it had been bought especially for him. And now the evening was falling; his uncle was finishing his jobs and clearing up and the quiet garden exuded a scent of after-rain.

And days like this would go on for ever. His mother would return and they would eat tea and... then it would be the 'bus home. And again next week his mother would bring him in the trolley 'bus. He suddenly remembered the sweets and took another out. But would it spoil the fish? He decided it would not and popped the sweet in his mouth. The front door bell was ringing; two hanging tubes striking together. He would go and let his mother in before his aunt got there.

But the little boy did not move. Nor did his uncle come in from the garden. The net curtains flapped again and the sun died in the evening stillness.. The gramophone, the sideboard of secrets, they had all gone. Only I remained in a room without mysteries or delights. The door bell was still ringing. I put aside the book which had fallen into my lap and rose to answer the door.

A Man in her Life

'Tell me about the man. The man you loved.'

The old woman smiled as she watched the shadow of an aeroplane pass across the ceiling of the ward.

'Who was he? What did he look like?'

At last the old woman spoke.

'He was tall. Good looking.' Her face creased and she laughed.

It had been good of Mrs Potts to come and see her. She seemed so interested: so kind.

But to Mrs Potts it had been one of many calls. The Friends of the Hospital arranged the visits - mostly to the old, always to the lonely.

The other patients found it difficult to make up their minds about the old woman. She was ninety nine and her main aim was to survive an operation on a cracked hip so that she would receive her telegram from The Queen.

This, of course, was laudable. They admired her courage which was considerable and her apparent lack of fear. But at first they found it difficult to reconcile their admiration with their reactions to her booming voice. She seemed to hear or notice nothing but what was going on around her bed. Even when two stretchers had been wheeled out, their occupants covered by a white sheet, she had continued to smile contentedly. Either she really did not notice or she was impervious to fears of the death which was so close to her.

But her loud voice, the result of many years talking to deaf friends, mostly her junior but all now departed, was seldom heard. Only when her visitor asked her about her past. Then, all heard. Everything which the old lady decided to impart was common knowledge in the ward.

There were times when one almost awaited a visitor's arrival to hear more shreds of the old lady's comfort. Ridiculous really, since her life had contained little of interest. But, like most reluctant lovers, her one short flirtation held more interest than all the affairs of a Casanova.

Sometimes her visitor would talk of other things and to routine questions she normally supplied monosyllabic answers.

The day of the operation was close when the minister called. She took his hand and said:

'I know I am old but would you pray for me?'

'Of course, of course. There is such power in prayer.'

'Because I want to…' she said as if people had doubted it: 'I want to live to be a hundred. It is good to live.'

The minister smiled and started to pray aloud while the old lady supplied responses.

When the minister had gone, the old lady received another visitor. She had never seen her before. The nurse escorted her to the old lady's bed.

'You must not tire her,' she said.

The old lady's eyes opened. Her eyes held a far away look. She seemed unconscious of her visitor's presence.

'Mrs Supple has told me about your young man,' said her visitor.

This was not quite true. The old lady had ventured no more information than that he was tall and good looking and Mrs Supple, her first visitor, had not remembered this. She had merely said: 'She likes to remember. Ask her about her young man.'

The old lady continued to stare straight ahead. Then another aeroplane cast its shadow in a curve across the ward. Her eyes followed it, and stayed staring at the ceiling. She could dimly hear someone talking: 'Was he handsome?'

Was who handsome? The old lady looked at her visitors noticing her for the first time. The question was repeated:

'Your young man; was he handsome?'

The old lady nodded.

'Yes, yes. Very tall. And handsome.'

'And when did you know him?'

'I was a gel. Only seventeen. Just a gel.'

'And did you like him?'

'Yes I liked him.'

'And you married him?'

'No,' she said, as if surprised at her own revelation. 'No I didn't marry him.'

'Why not?'

The old lady looked puzzled, then smiled.

'Because he never asked me.'

The visitor sat back on her chair, thinking of something to say which would bring comfort. But it was not needed. It was too long ago to give pain. And the old lady was staring at the ceiling again.

A nurse touched her visitor on the arm.

'I think perhaps... if you leave her.'

The visitor nodded.

'She will sleep now.'

The curtains flapped against the large windows, casting moving shadows across the beds. The warm spell continued, emphasising the clinical atmosphere of the ward.

The old lady had awoken early. It seemed that she had things to do. Long before the bed pans were slid into place and the mobile patients flapped to the bathrooms and toilets, she had begun to prepare herself for the day to come.

At last she opened her eyes and waved her hand at a nurse. A few moments elapsed, then the nurse came to her bedside, anxious to continue her duties.

The old lady had long since ceased to recognise the need for haste. For some moments she smiled, looking not at the nurse but at the flapping curtains. The nurse began to move away. Then the old lady spoke.

'Has Andrew been told?'

The strange question arrested the nurse's departure.

'Andrew?'

'He is in my Sunday School class.'

The nurse smiled.

'Oh, well I'm sure he has been told.'

She pulled the old lady's bed cover further round her as if to compensate for her enforced inactivity.

'But has he been told I am alright. Does he know it is all over?'

The nurse said:

51

'All over?'

'The operation. All over.'

The nurse again tugged at the quilt and smiled, saying briskly:

'Not quite Not quite over. We'll tell him tomorrow.'

But the old lady's strange request remained with the nurse after the bustle of the morning had passed. She watched her last visitor before the operation leaving her bedside and spoke to her.

'Did she say about a boy, Andrew?'

The visitor nodded.

'She spoke more than she has ever done to me. She gave a description of the man she loved - or liked as she says. He can only have been a boy. Tall, dark, good looking. She was very detailed. What he wore, how he walked; his way of smiling.'

'And - the boy. Is he known?'

'He is in her Sunday School class. He seems to have a greater attraction for her than the others.'

The window cleaner rested his ladder against the wall of the hospital. There was no need for him to be there: the hospital was not part of his round, but no one would notice him. No one questioned the right of a window cleaner to be anywhere.

He slung his cloth over the top rung of the ladder and deposited his bucket on the ground.

The weather was still warm. He wiped the sweat from his forehead and rolled a cigarette; then, leaving his ladder, walked towards the hospital entrance. As he passed through the Victorian colonnade he stopped, threw down his cigarette and removed his hat. There was nothing to stop him entering a hospital.

When he reached the top of the stairs, he turned towards one of the wards. On seeing a nurse, he indicated towards the ward.

'Can I go in?' he said.

She indicated the visiting times pinned to the wall.

'Not really. Do you have a relative there?'

'Sort of,' he said. 'The old lady. She was...' The nurse smiled.

'I'm sorry I'm afraid you can't see her.'

The window cleaner's face clouded. He turned away, ashamed of the tears in his eyes.

Then he felt the nurse's hand on his arm. 'She's resting. She's very weak,' she said.

'So she's...'

'Alive. Not quite kicking but she will be.'

The window cleaner laughed aloud, then stopped. This was not the place for frivolity

'Can I wait?' he said.

'She may be some time, but yes you can wait.'

Inside the ward the evening shadows were long across the beds. The sun had moved down behind the trees giving merely a reddish tinge to the evening. The old lady appeared to be sleeping. In fact she was awake. For a strongly religious lady she, surprisingly, had no fears; nothing weighed heavily upon her conscience. What had happened all those years ago was a secret between two people. She was glad of this. She was glad that, at the time, everything had been hushed up and settled to the satisfaction of her strictly moral family, her barren sister and her errant lover.

Her only thoughts were for the little boy in her Sunday School class and for the man who, unbeknown to her, was patiently rolling another cigarette in the small alcove outside the ward. Her great but hidden fear that she should not see them again had receded. Her gratitude that, when she again faced that long dark tunnel from which she had emerged triumphant, the blood that she had bequeathed to a little boy eighty years ago would live on in her great grandson. And in her great great grandson. The little boy in her Sunday school class.

Fast Runs the River

Boleyn watched the sweet papers flow downstream and under the bridge. Later he would go up to the church and see them as they cascaded into the small pool under the spinney. He knew just how long they would take to reach that point; he had their journey timed to a minute.

The last one, he thought, will be reaching the graveyard.

Boleyn took a large bag from his pocket and extracted another sweet. He did not mind which flavour; the flavour mattered less than the colour of the wrapping and this must be used in strict rotation. He stuffed a lemon sweet in his mouth and tossed the paper into the water. Then he hoisted his satchel onto his shoulder and cut across the grass to the spinney.

'They'll be at the gate,' he sang. 'They'll be at the gate an' I'm beatin''em.' His satchel swung as he ran, and his cap slid further down the side of his head. When it fell off, he picked it up and stuffed it into his pocket.

'If I don't hurry they'll be at the spinney and... Oh! Cripes, I've only got a minute.'

But he arrived in time - as he always did. Then he sat and looked upstream for the first sweet paper to arrive. He took out his cap and stirred the water with it. They still didn't show.

There should be a red one due now, he thought. Raspberry it was. Always raspberry first.

Boleyn sighed.

'It's got stuck. Darn the raspberry - It's got stuck.'

He knew now that, unless the current released the red paper from its bondage, he would have to wait for an orange coloured wrapper. But the orange wrapper did not come. He dabbled his cap in the stream so that the sunlight broke its surface into tiny gems. But still no wrappers came.

'I got 'ere on time. They must be 'ere.'

Boleyn began to walk along the bank towards the bridge. He must follow the course of the river. He passed through the gate of the churchyard and into that quiet place where, every day, his bits of paper floated past the disinterested occupants. Every day but this, that is, for there was no sign of any papers now.

Then his keen young eyes caught sight of one.

'Green!' But he ate lime sixth. 'Where were the other five?'

He walked towards the paper but stopped suddenly. A hand had reached from behind a tombstone, snatched the paper, and withdrawn.

At first Boleyn was inclined to run away. Then he saw a flash of white material behind the hand as it darted into the water to pick out another paper.

'Brown! It's old Brown. What's 'e playin' at,' muttered Boleyn. Brown often watched the papers go by. But as Boleyn peered round he could see that it was not Brown. The girl he looked at was very different from Brown. She was neither old nor wrinkled. Boleyn thought that she was very pretty.

Without turning round, the girl spoke:

'I thought you would come. Come here and sit beside me.'

Boleyn stared.

'Come on. Tell me about your sweet papers. Do you know how to time them?'

Boleyn nodded.

'Stop nodding as if your head was loose. Come and sit beside me.'

She patted the mound beside her.

Boleyn sank uncertainly to the ground and sat beside the girl, ill at ease.

'Now, could you show me how the papers go?'

Boleyn nodded.

'Where do they go?'

'Downstream.'

'That's not very surprising is it? Where do they go after the spinney?'

'I'm the only one that knows besides Brown.'

'That's why I'm asking you. It goes underground doesn't it?'

Boleyn nodded.

'Into the school grounds?'

'Yes.'

'Where I can't go?'

Boleyn agreed.

'Will you tell me where?'

Boleyn was about to tell her. Then he checked himself.

'For a price,' he said.

'Oh you cheeky boy. I'll buy you all the sweets you like.'

'I don't want sweets. I want two things.'

'Well?'

'I want ter know why you want the information.'

'I can't tell you that. A little boy...!'

'Then I can't tell you.'

Boleyn had lost his nervousness. He was beginning to enjoy himself. As he watched the girl stretch her naked sun-browned legs, he took out his cap and began to screw it between his hands.

'You see,' he said, 'It's obviously a bloke in the school in' it? And you want ter get messages to 'im.'

The girl stared in disbelief.

'It's bin done before,' he said and then regretted that he had disclaimed any brilliant powers of deduction.

'It's bin done before but the girl's gone. Only we know now.'

'I don't know.'

'Brown and me knows.'

'Well tell me. I do want to send messages but the caretaker must never find out.'

'Who is he first? Who'll you be sendin' messages: to?'

'Paul.'

'Paul who?'

'Paul Evers.'

It seemed reasonable. He was a big chap. Very handsome, Boleyn supposed, to a girl like her. He nodded. Yeah, he would do it.

'And the second thing you wanted?' the girl asked.

'A kiss. A kiss from you.'

The girl stared again.

'A k-kiss?'

56

'Yes.'

The girl sat back and sighed.

'Oh very well.' She stood up taking his hand in hers. 'Show me where it goes,' she said.

Boleyn showed her where the stream went underground below the spinney and made a map of where it cut the school boundary so that Paul Evers could be ready for the messages as they passed.

It was a week later when Boleyn kept his appointment with the girl at the tombstone where they had first met. He was a little nervous for he had never kissed a girl before, certainly never a girl of her age or beauty. She bent over him and took his face in her hands.

'There,' she said, kissing him gently on the lips.

Boleyn sighed. He wondered how she kissed Paul. It would take longer, Boleyn decided, much longer. And she would whisper words such as she had written in the notes Boleyn had read as they came sailing past the copse before they reached the part of the river at which Paul Evers would wait for them. He mused on how easy it would be to trap a girl. Well, easy for someone like himself. Why, she had even asked him to design a yellow box in which to send the messages! And he was glad he hadn't told the girl who Brown was. If she had known that he was the caretaker! But she did not. Nor did she know of the laughter she occasioned from the old man when he read her notes.

The sun cast skeletal patterns of branches on the ivied walls of the school. Boleyn walked towards them feeling that he had earned more than a kiss that day. He had earned an unending supply of loving messages. Instead of Paul's name at the top he would imagine his own and the kiss which he could still feel on his lips would be there in his memory if he ever doubted their sincerity.

And behind him in the churchyard the girl remained. She waited until the boy had disappeared and then hurried round the school to where the stream re-emerged from the boundary of its grounds. Here she intently watched the water. Then her hand flashed out and she pulled to the bank a small piece of polystyrene. Bits like this were common; they floated down from the factory where they were disgorged as waste.

But only one piece per day bore a blue cross - and it was such a piece that the girl now held.

Gently she flipped open the box and looked inside, She gave a quick glance round but she was alone. She looked at her watch. One o'clock. She must be quick. She gave the note no more than a passing glance before sliding it into her pocket and running towards the shops.

'Roving Lad,' she muttered. 'Two thirty. Kempton.'

In Memory of Sally Howard

'See that, boy? See that heart?'

I could see an elaborately carved heart and in it the name Sally.

'Did you do that, Grandpa?' I asked.

'Nearly sixty years ago I made that heart, boy. And it lives as a reminder to me of the only girl I ever really loved.'

'But Grandpa,' I protested, 'this seat is newly painted, it is painted every year.'

'And I,' replied my Grandfather, 'come along every year and re-new that heart.

'It's cut deep as you can see - all I have to do is scrape away the paint.' I looked at the old man with renewed interest and wondered who Sally was - a girl who could inspire such undying devotion.

'She lived at Howard Hall,' he said, as if answering my thoughts, 'but I must tell you first what the town looked like then. Take a deep breath of sea air boy and remember that all this happened before these gardens even were built.'

'But the seat...'

'Was here before the gardens. It was the only seat on the front.'

I looked at the rows of identical seats and I could see that this was slightly different from all the rest.

He swept his cap off, as if it were an act of respect to the heroine of his story, and wiped an arm across his sweating forehead. Then he took me back sixty years to a time when none of the promenade hotels existed; when the pier was merely a broken down landing stage and the beach was empty save for the boats and the fishermen mending their nets. Only the double crescent of Regency houses were as they stand today; I reflected that this was then a pleasure ground for the rich only and that the poor were too busy earning their meagre living to think themselves picturesque in their little fishermen's hovels.

As soon as one took the road out of town one reached open

country and, as the road progressed, the cultivated patches were replaced by open fields and these, in their turn, by a broad belt of forest. It was deep in that forest that the Howards lived their isolated lives in a fashion undreamt of by even the richest of the town dwellers. For generations after the family had acquired its industrial fortune, it had occupied this house - so remote from the Howards' native north - acquiring the reputation of landed gentry - a reputation based on the family's name which was shared by the previous aristocratic owners of the house with whom, hard as they tried, the Howards could establish no claim of kinship.

Augustus Howard had a reputation as a great romantic, acquired through this purchase of his namesake's property, but the reputation was false. He had moved south because he was an upstart in the north and he conducted his business from this distance with a hard headed exactness which left his underlings in no doubt as to his lack of romance.

The first romantic Howard was the result of an odd marriage. It was the union of Jeremiah Howard with the daughter of an up and coming London merchant which produced the Sally of my grandfather's story.

The marriage, from the point of view of Jeremiah Howard, was a miserable failure: his wife's father did not fulfil his early promise and his wife proved no compensation to the industrialist - producing as she did a daughter whose liking for romance and addiction to sentimental novels bode ill for the future.

'I used to see her, boy,' said my grandfather, 'when I went to cut wood for my father. It was a good bit further than I need have gone for wood but it wasn't known why I went there. And I always came back with a good supply. Sally used to meet me at the gates of Howard Hall and we'd walk all round the rusting palings which were the park's boundary. There were always so many weeds and Sally used to pick the little wild flowers and even treasured buttercups and daises, and she'd pick dandelions and take them home. In the spring she used to look out for crocuses and snowdrops but she would never pick them - she liked to see them growing under the trees and in clumps of green grass; she couldn't understand why I ignored them. Perhaps she was so tired of her wealth that simple things made more of an impression.

'Anyway, I met her like that for about a year and, on my seventeenth birthday, your great grandfather died and I took over the shop. It was a big responsibility but I enjoyed it and soon I'd almost forgotten about Sally. Then one day her father came into the shop and waited until all the other customers had left before taking me by the arm and steering me towards a little room back of the shop. I don't know how he knew it was there but he seemed to. He seemed to know everything.

'He told me he had something serious to discuss with me and I felt it an honour - not even allayed when he said he thought Sally was expecting a baby. He called it a "happy event" but, from his expression, I could tell that he wasn't really happy about it. He never actually said that I was responsible but, being seventeen and a virgin of unbelievable innocence, I felt very manly and relished the thought that a man of his status should accuse me of committing such a delightful crime!

'So when he suggested - and he never so much as stated one fact - that I should fulfil my obligations towards Sally, I gladly accepted the blame and prepared for the wedding. But the wedding never came, as Jeremiah Howard never intended that it should; instead I agreed to take Sally on as a partner and her father glibly talked about "future nuptials" as if he were talking of going to the moon. Neither did the baby ever come and I believe now that Sally had never been expecting one.

'I left the business arrangements to Mr Howard which was about the silliest thing I ever did in my life and, by the time I was twenty, Sally had complete control of the shop and I was nothing more than a counter assistant. I wondered why a man with his money hadn't undertaken to set Sally up in some other type of business but Sally told me frankly that his fortunes had been on the wane and that he had taken a fancy to the shop as the "sort of thing his romantic daughter would take to".

'And the plan worked. A young man with big ideas married her and, when the old man died, the couple received a good amount to expand their business. And, of course, they took over Howard Hall which, during her father's period of financial trouble, Sally thought would have to be sold.

'It was then that I reflected on her father's plan - how he had secured his daughter's security without spending a penny, but I thought also of Sally. She was not happy and had never been really happy about the shop. As business boomed and her husband bought himself into other and bigger concerns, Sally's interest in me returned. I don't know what made me start walking towards the woods again, perhaps it was a hankering after the youth I had lost and a time when I had been happy. I did not resent Sally's part in my downfall and I took to walking with her again and she showed the same interest in the wild flowers that she had always done. Then the war came and her husband was killed. I hoped for her hand; I hoped also for re-instatement in your great grandfather's business. But it never came. Sally could only appreciate wild flowers when she had riches to scorn. So she married another business man and, by the time the second war came, Howard Hall had returned to its original splendour. The grounds were extended and the wooded paths we used to walk in were replaced by formal gardens.

'Then her second husband died but this time, although I was willing, I was given no chance to renew the acquaintance and, anyway, I was married by then... happily,' he said as an afterthought.

Then my grandfather stood up and looked wistfully at the heart.

'I always forgave her,' he said, 'and I still...,' he hesitated, 'and I still think of her. Not easy to forget her when I see her every day.'

'Every day?' I asked, surprised.

I followed his eyes to a grocery shop which bore the name Howard's. 'But my father never told me,' I said.

'No, your father never knew. If he had been a more observant man he might have noticed my visits to that shop and seen me talking to old Mother Howard. Old Mother Howard is...'

He turned to face me. He did not need to finish his sentence. He sat down again and began to talk as if nothing had happened - as if this most important story had not been told.

'What will the sixties bring do you think, boy?' he asked

I told him that I thought they'd bring happiness to those that deserved it. It was a silly thing to say and my grandfather thought so too, but I had been very much affected by his story.

When I left him I walked several times around the block before coming back to Howard's the grocers. I don't remember what I bought; I think perhaps it was potatoes, but the reason for my visit was to ask for Mother Howard. I don't remember exactly what I asked her but I do re-member her answer. She told me she had never heard of my grandfather and that she had never lived in Howard Hall. I had expected her to deny the story and, as I looked out of the grocer's window at my grandfather, I felt how badly he had been betrayed. As I watched the old man, I saw him pointing to the heart carved into the green seat on which we had been sitting. A stranger's eyes followed the direction of his finger.

I let them talk for some half an hour; then my grandfather left the seat and I walked towards it. It was only as I approached the seat from the shops that I noticed the barely discernible plate on the back of the seat. It read:

'This seat was placed here in memory of Sally Howard who died June 1st 1949.'

How I Love You Mary Southern

I had never looked closely at the stones, not until that June morning when I went to play as usual in the churchyard. David was there, as ever, waiting for me.

He beckoned and led me between the tombs to the mausoleum, where he stopped.

'Joanna Southern. Aged 11 years,' he read. I looked at the inscription.

'My sister,' he said.

I felt there must have been many years between them because of the weathering of the stone, although I could not decipher the Roman numerals which recorded the date of entombment. I was surprised when David recounted facts of her life and told me how they had played together as young children.

When David talked of his sister that day there were tears in his eyes but, although he told me incidents of her life, he said nothing of her death, and I put this down to an unwillingness to recreate scenes which were still vivid enough to give him pain. But then he brightened quite suddenly and took my hand again, leading me over the tufted grass to a marble tomb which bore the words:

'MAJOR DENNIS HAPGOOD. LATE OF THIS PARISH.'

Underneath was a pious verse and a date almost entirely obscured by the grass.

'The major used to sit me on his knee,' David said, 'and tell me stories I can still remember.'

I was eager to hear the major's stories and David was able to recall them in great detail. In fact I have thought it best to recount one of them as the major would have told it because the childish narration that I heard was so poignant that my memory will never let it go.

'I was a soldier then, and we marched into Devon with all the pride of a victorious regiment - which we were. We were billeted on the people of a small Devon village - I will not tell you the name because my story reflects little credit on its inhabitants - and I found myself in the home of a merchant whose three daughters were most taken by my uniform; I attribute their admiration to this and not to my person, not out of modesty, but because even the meanest of the regiment found admirers in this way.

'One of the daughters was Mary and I felt for her an intense admiration - I hesitate to say that I loved her - but when her father arranged for her a marriage with a wealthy but elderly gentleman I felt a great disappointment which was in no way decreased when I saw the bent old man leading her, or rather being led by her, from the village church.

'I suppose Mary's father was not alone in hoping for the death of this man and, when it came, there was a great deal of suspicion as to the manner of it. But none of the blame rested on Mary and she was subsequently married to a middle aged merchant in the town named Southern and, again, I perceived that the marriage was none of her choice.

'By this time I had returned to the village after a campaign abroad for the regiment was to be stationed more permanently in Devon where we were to help defend the country against the threatened French invasion. I used to meet Mary Southern when she came home and we took to walking together in the fields. I can remember how she used to hold her dress to prevent the morning dew spoiling the hem and how I kissed her and she blushed, saying that she was a married woman.

'But my forwardness did not diminish her liking for me and we continued our walks. I did not kiss her again until about a year later when our love making went further than a kiss.

'The event was followed by the poisoning of Mary's husband.

'For the first time stories circulated concerning the circumstances of her first husband's death although, at the time, I attached no importance to them. But I was obsessed with the idea that she had killed for my sake and rushed to the prison to try to help her.

'I found her incarcerated in a small dark cell and, as I picked my way towards her, I did so through an inch of water. The cell stank of her own filth and frequent scamperings told me that we were not the sole occupants of the room. She told me that she had not killed her husband but, at the time, I did not believe her. She also told me that, whatever happened at her trial, she would not die because she was expecting a child; "a special child", she told me, "the child of our love".

'At her trial Mary Southern was found guilty of murder but pleaded her belly to good effect. However the delay did nothing to soften the hearts of her accusers and she was committed to a death cell, more ugly than the first, and there she suffered the pain of childbirth alone. I was not allowed to be with her and I prayed that she might die. But she did not do so and, remarkably also, the child lived to be taken into the Southern household. There it was brought up with its half sister, the female child of Mary's second ill-fated marriage.

'After the birth the order of execution was given and I was permitted one last visit to my lover's cell. It is an occasion I still remember vividly, still think about constantly and still dream about at night when there are no other matters to divert my mind. She was lying, pale and shrunken on a wooden bench which acted as a bed and, as I spoke to her, it was difficult to realise that she was only eighteen and a child of beauty not a year before. She did not move, nor did she speak, just listened and smiled as I voiced my undying love for her. Then, as an officer came to take me away, she whispered: "I am innocent", and for the first time I believed her.

'In a week her scarcely living body was carried to a place outside the town where gladiators had fought in Roman times. It was a huge amphitheatre which I believed had been built long before the Romans came to Britain and this was to be the last entertainment performed there. I paid the executioner well to make an end of her before she was tied in the midst of the faggots.

'Before the flames had made an end of her, I walked away from the amphitheatre, sick with grief, looking for an opportunity to end my own life. But I realised I could do more for Mary alive; I could take her child - our child - and lavish on it and the daughter of Mary's marriage all the love which I felt for their mother.

'For nine years I lived on in the village in a cottage I had built in the fields where Mary and I had walked and it was during this time that

I forced a confession of the murder of Mary's husbands from the father who had gained so much from their deaths. But, at the end of those nine years, Mary's first child died and, six years after, her half brother followed her to the grave.'

The day following David's account of the major's story, I was prevented from going to the churchyard. Instead I went with my mother into the town to help her carry home our provisions. But, that evening, I slipped out of the house when all were asleep and crossed the lane to the churchyard gates. When I reached them I found that a padlock secured the latch and I walked around the railed section to a low wall I knew I could climb. Here I pulled myself up with the help of the low, hanging branches of a tree and crouched on the wall ready to leap down if all was clear.

But I heard voices. I pulled my coat tighter around me and strained into the darkness to catch any words of the conversation which should float towards me. But the voices had stopped. I remained perfectly still, knowing the talkers had observed my presence. I could feel their eyes upon me.

But my courage did not desert me. I eased myself down onto the ledge of the wall and, placing my foot on the top of a flat tomb, gently dropped to the ground below.

Still there was no noise but the faint rustling of the wind in the trees and the monotonous hooting of owls in the nearby wood. I made my way between the gravestones, until I came to a large white tomb which, even in the dark, I recognised as one on which a massive white angel stood guard. It was then that I saw the eyes.

They were no more than slits as they stared out of the dark at me from behind the tomb. I was too frightened to move and just stared at the eyes staring back at me. In a moment I was knocked back as the cat to whom the eyes belonged sprang at me.

For a few moments I sat where I had tumbled to the earth. The cat had run off, but I had been severely shaken and, as I picked myself up, I heard the first drops of rain falling on the leaves and made my way quickly to the Southern vault.

I could discern two figures. One of them I recognised as David, the other was standing in the shadow of the vault. I approached and, as

I did so, David's companion moved behind the tomb and was lost to sight. Then David turned. But his face was not as I remembered it; he was angry at my intrusion. I made to go but he called to me and, when I turned back, he was scrabbling in the earth, seemingly making no impression upon it. Then I saw that he was indicating something to me. I knelt down and pulled away the turfs from the wall of the vault.

The inscription was one which I dreaded to see. But even my childish mind had already considered the implications of the major's story. I looked up. David had gone and I was left alone in the graveyard. I took one last look at the inscription before replacing the turfs. I read:

'DAVID: BROTHER OF THE ABOVE.'

And ran to the low wall by which I should escape from this place of the living dead.

The Last Hour with Davinia

Whenever I hear bees buzzing in a hot sunny garden, I recall that lazy, blissful summer's day when I drank beer in the garden of the Sugarloaf and looked into the eyes of the most beautiful girl I had ever met.

It hadn't been a hot summer, so the sun was doubly welcome - and essential somehow to our last meeting. I remember how she ran her long fingers up the stem of her glass and promised to keep in touch. I knew she wouldn't. Perhaps she knew too. Certainly we both knew that we must enjoy the hour. For it would never come again.

The barman was busying himself collecting glasses - a kind of artificial energy had overcome him, knowing there was more important and pressing work to be done in the bar. He smiled at Davinia. Everyone smiled at Davinia.

Davinia was about twenty three, reasonably tall, but somehow difficult to adequately describe. Strange that after all these years I can picture her but not describe her. Her hair was not blonde, not dark... unexceptional. I cannot describe her legs - so often did she wear long dresses. But her face was beautiful and her personality carried her through life on a wave of adulation - and envy.

And the barman had waited to clean down a table and to pass the time of day. He was using up valuable time - my time. My last hour with Davinia.

Davinia smiled. Her words were irrelevant and commonplace. She spoke of parties to which I had not been invited and the small legacy which had allowed her to start a new life in the West Country: her prospects; her hopes...

I spoke of the dim hallway in which we had met every week for the past two years - prosaic, platonic meetings at which I could never let my love for her show.

I told her how I would miss those meetings; she said I would find someone else. Which showed her knowledge of my feelings - she knew I should find no one like her.

Odd that I had often been surly and irritable. She must have thought me a strange suitor - if suit was the correct word to describe our friendship.

She sipped from her glass and returned it to the white metal table before her. The air was absolutely still and the traffic on the London Road could have been many miles away.

Davinia smiled.

'Would you like another drink?'

I collected her glass and made to rise.

'Not for me,' she said, placing her hand over the glass. 'For you.'

I knew she meant it. She had no head for it.

I quickly bought another for myself cursing the queue and the barman's indolence.

When I returned she did not look at me. It was as if I had never left.

I lifted my mug and motioned:

'Cheers.'

She smiled.

'Just half an hour.'

It seemed impossible that I should never see her again.

She said nothing of what we had meant to each other - if indeed I had meant anything to her. If, deep under the inconsequential conversation, there was a fondness for me - I should never know it. And if there was she knew better than to express it.

The station was crowded with coastward bound holiday makers. We stood for a few moments unspeaking, embarrassed. Then the train came. Strangely, I welcomed it. The final farewell would have some meaning; the silence did not.

She opened the train door and then she put one arm round my shoulder and kissed me hard on the mouth.

Of all the contact I had had with women that was the most sensuous moment I had known. I felt I should do something in return. I couldn't speak - just looked at her gratefully - like a small boy given a valued gift.

Then I bent towards her and she kissed me again - without this time making any other contact.

'I won't wait at the window.'

I nodded. It would have been an anticlimax to watch her arm waving from the window and the train disappearing to a speck on the track.

God, how I wished to hold her; to tell her I loved her. To kiss her.

She closed the carriage door and I walked up the long stairway from the platform.

The man at the ticket barrier laughed. Whatever he thought wasn't true. He may have thought that we were lovers; that she would return to me soon.

He may have thought me happy for I must have retained that goodbye smile and the memory of a kiss. But it was not so: I had spent my last hour with Davinia.

The Snowman Approaches

Christmas had come and gone without the snow which would have given it a bit of colour. Instead a strong north wind had thrown the teeming rain into our faces and our traditional Christmas Day walk had been reduced to a brisk walk around the block.

But now the snow had come; now that life was back to normal after the festivities. Now that it could hamper road travel, delay the trains and disrupt the racing programme. I watched it falling. Pretty white flakes against a darkening background of approaching dusk. Perhaps it would be gone by morning.

But it had not gone by morning. As I pulled back the bedroom curtains, it was still falling and a three or four inch carpet of snow covered the earth. Along the fences, against which the snow had drifted, the depth was about a foot.

I sat back on the bed and rubbed my tired eyes. My wife was still sleeping and there was no movement in my daughter's room. It was then that I heard the sound I had dreaded. The telephone.

I ran down the stairs and lifted the receiver before it awoke the household.

'Hello.'

'Mr Beech?'

I nodded stupidly as if he could see me.

'I have given you a long time to pay, Mr Beech. I think we have been very lenient.'

'Very lenient,' I gabbled, 'you've been very kind. I need just a few more weeks.'

'No more weeks, Mr Beech, I'm afraid.'

'But...'

'I *am* very sorry Mr Beech' (he emphasised the 'am' as if he expected me to disbelieve his sincerity). 'However I must call a halt to this business. I want the money by next weekend.'

He did not sound sorry. It sounded as if he would prefer if I did not pay. I shuddered at the thought of what would happen if I did not pay.

I thought carefully.

'There are securities. I could provide...' There was a click. 'Hello, hello,' I shouted into the mouthpiece. But he obviously wasn't interested in securities.

'Hell,' I said and replaced the receiver. I walked into the kitchen, boiled a kettle and watched the snow drifting down as I waited for the tea to draw.

The sounds of children's laughter drifted down the street, echoing from the walls of the warehouses opposite. For an hour I shovelled snow into a heap where my daughter patted and fashioned the heap into a snowman.

'Daddy. Twigs; we must use twigs.'

'Twigs?'

'You put twigs round and it cements the snow inside and then you cover the frame with snow.'

It seemed unlikely, but I laughed and waited until she had brought sticks and made a frame of them. There seemed to be more sticks than snow. However I had to admit that it made a fine snowman.

We used a casserole dish for the snowman's hat, a carrot as his nose and two large flat oval stones for his eyes. Perhaps the stones were a mistake. It made the snowman's face look skull-like with two empty sockets where eyes should have been.

And even after my daughter had added buttons, a scarf and a cheery smile, he was not the snowman of the Christmas card. He was a creature of the fast approaching night.

The telephone rang again. I answered it dreading that it would be the man again. It was not. I mounted the stairs, looking in on my daughter. She was asleep - and smiling.

I walked into the bedroom taking a last look at the garden before drawing the curtains. It was strange; I thought that the snowman had been built further back, further away from the house. I laughed. How absurd. I laughed so loudly that my wife was awoken.

'Brian?'

'It's alright. Go to sleep.'

'But you laughed?'

Yes. I had laughed. Was that so strange?

It was during that night that the noises began. Strange groans that could have been the wind, creaks that could have been the furniture, and footsteps that could have been - and probably were - my imagination.

And sleep did not comfort me for I dreamt. I could hear a telephone ringing. In my sleep I answered it and the man was always on the other end. 'I am sorry Mr Beech,' he said. 'I am sorry Mr Beech.'

But the dreams passed and morning came.

I put on the kettle and opened the kitchen door to empty the grouts. It was as I opened the back door that I saw it. The snowman.

The snowman, his sinister skull-face staring at me. And he was closer to the house.

I retreated into the house and slammed the door. I passed a hand across my brow. Absurdly I was sweating. In the early morning cold, I was sweating.

I breathed deeply, clutched the tea pot as if it were a weapon and went out into the garden again. I calmly emptied the grouts and returned to make the tea.

But I did not look at the snowman.

The telephone rang. I picked it up, trembling. 'Yes,' I would have the money by Friday evening. 'Yes, I realised what would happen if I did not.'

If I paid the money back which I had stolen from the firm nothing more would be said. If I did not he would tell the police. He would not believe I had just borrowed it, intending to pay it back. He was being very kind in giving me the opportunity to save myself from imprisonment.

Why had I taken it? Why had the horse lost? Why was I such a fool? Why was the snowman closing in on me?

I took up the tea. My daughter snuggled happily into our bed deriving warmth from her mother. I took a last look at the garden but could not see the snowman. He must be approaching the house now.

Oh Christ.

It was Monday night. The telephones rang throughout my dreams and, when I awoke, the wailing and creaking noises of the night assailed my ears. They were coming from the garden. Oh God, they were coming from the garden. Why could not my wife hear? Why could not my daughter hear? Could they not see what was happening to the snowman? How he had taken on life to haunt me.

And on Tuesday I had no sleep. Nor on Wednesday. Thursday passed, my tormentor now just under my window and my sleeping and waking nights tormented by his howls.

Friday.

Drip. Drip. There was a cry as of one in pain.

I rushed to the window knowing it to be the snowman.

I looked down. Down to a pile of sticks immediately under my window. The absurdity of it struck me. I even looked up to see if the snowman had scaled the wall and was waiting to pounce. There was no snowman. There were large patches of green grass where the snow had been. The snow was melting.

The telephone rang. I had no answer for the man. I didn't have the money. I began to cry as I picked up the receiver.

'Yes?'

A voice said 'Mr Beech?' It knew I was Mr Beech.

'Yes,' I said.

'Mr Beech. Your deadline has arrived.'

'I haven't got it,' I screamed. 'I tried to get it...'

'I have it Mr Beech.'

'You have it? But...'

'I have the money you gave to Mr Ellsworth to put on Likely Lad in the 3.30 at Kempton.'

'You have it?' I repeated stupidly.

'Mr Ellsworth is not completely stupid, Mr Beech, and nor am I. He returned the money to me and it has been safely returned where you got it from. Why did you not tell me you could not pay your bills, Mr Beech?'

'I don't know. There was so much owing...'

'And you thought betting was an answer - you a man who had never betted in his life?'

'How did you know?'

'Why else would you give the money to someone else to place your bet? Certainly not so that you would not be seen placing a bet because Mr Ellsworth would always inform the police that he had placed it on your behalf.'

'Yes.'

'You had never been to a betting shop.'

'No.'

'And now you probably never will. Because you will come to see me and we will discuss your financial problems. We will find a way out of them.'

I agreed. Dumbly I put down the receiver and walked into the garden, needing air. I looked at the pile of sticks on the patio and remembered vaguely my daughter collecting them and placing them roughly in the position where they now lay.

The Friday Evening Library

My stints at Langridge Library took place on a Friday evening, when I worked until eight, and my two hours there were a peaceful interlude during a hard day. I enjoyed my cycle ride to Langridge - the most far flung of the branches housed in a church hall on the edge of the Langridge housing estate. I also enjoyed the company of Jock, the caretaker. I had never discovered why Jock's presence was necessary there but the church authorities deemed it so. Certainly, if any trouble had been started by the youths on the estate, this kindly and amenable old man would have been unable to deal with it.

Most of our time at Langridge Library was spent in conversation, and only very occasionally would we be bothered by a reader. Jock had been a footballer in his young days and regaled me with stories about his exploits. Presumably most of them had been embellished over the years but there is no doubt that he believed them to be true. But by the time half past six arrived his main thought was to be 'off home', and he would exhort the clock hand to 'get up the hill' to seven o'clock. Seven for me meant a ride back to the central library and a return to more arduous work and I was content for the last half hour to go slowly.

I was not sure how the presence of a branch library at Langridge had been justified, and I wonder how much business the mobile library which has replaced it now does. But those readers we had enjoyed the facilities and were able to chose from a variety of good new books, since there was no rush to remove the new Agatha Christie or Barbara Cartland from the shelves.

The majority of readers were elderly and would dump their returning books on the counter without a word to me and walk over to Jock to enjoy an exchange of local news. It was not rudeness, just a recognition of priorities and they would always be most appreciative when they came to leave and deposited their newly selected books on the counter. Some even referred to Jock as the Librarian and would ask his advice on books - not always an unwise move since he had read most of the thrillers and westerns in the library and his wife had read the romances. There was little else.

When we did have visits from people under sixty, it was rarely to borrow books. A stranger would ask the way to Mitcham, or a youth would wander in to show his disgust of the establishment he considered we represented. Perhaps the combination of church, local authority and learning (for reading was considered such) invited such feelings.

There was one shelf of children's books but we did not, as you might have expected, cater for children. So when a collection of scruffy urchins arrived one day it was an unusual occurrence.

' 'Allo.'

I smiled uncertainly at the leader of the gang who could only have been eight at the most.

'I want a book.'

I smiled again, encouraged, and took a walk to the shelves - unusual exercise at Langridge.

My visitors watched while I scanned the shelf. Most of the children's books were dirty and tattered. Most were unsuitable. This young rough would not be satisfied with Beatrix Potter or Janet and John. The happy ordered life of Jane and Peter would be anathema to him. Far better to capture his imagination. I grabbed two scruffy books - one on smugglers and another of space adventures.

I took them to the boys hurriedly because I felt that they had really completed their adventure by entering the library's portals and would as soon be out.

I perched in front of them on a stool - the library's only furniture.

'There are two here. They're a bit tatty - but we can always get more down from Hennor Park. Nice new books with exciting stories, I promise.'

'Have you got any with bare ladies in?' asked their leader seriously.

I thought for a moment.

'You like ladies do you?'

'Only bare ones.'

I hated to discourage him but could not present the library as a source of girlie pictures.

'Bare ones?' I said, stalling.

'Like you see on the news stands.'

'I know,' I said.

'They won't sell them mags to us.'

I showed surprise.

'No. Well 'ave you got 'ny?'

I had to admit we didn't. I felt their parents would not have thanked me for supplying them with nude books from the art section which were normally only issued 'on application to staff'.

'But there's this one on smugglers.'

'Oh,' said the leader without interest.

'And, look at this,' I said, thrusting the tatty book on space travel forward: *Adventures in Space.*

'Monsters?'

'I should think so.'

He grabbed the book from me.'

'No monsters,' he said disgustedly and dropped the book to the floor.

The boy was providing a challenge and his mates, I knew, would follow wherever he led. If he joined the library so would they. If he tore down the bookshelves, then so would they. But I prided myself on my judgement of character and I was sure this lad was good material. I was certain he would enjoy the adventures reading would bring and he had the future of his friends in his hands. I was further convinced there was no malice in him - impishness in plenty but no malice.

But his next remark, I must admit, discouraged me.

'So no bare ladies then. Don't you like bare ladies?'

'Well yes I do,' I admitted.

'Well why ain't you got 'em then?'

This stumped me for a moment.

'Well you can't read bare ladies can you?' I eventually answered lamely. We both knew the answer was inadequate and I had failed him. Libraries just could not provide what the public wanted. He started to move away.

'Smugglers,' I said pathetically.

He turned round in wonderment. Clearly librarians were not

only inadequate in supplying required material, but their behaviour branded them as lunatics.

'This book on smugglers,' I shouted. 'It has some blood-curdling tales.'

It must have been the word blood that arrested him. He turned round. I made a desperate fling to retain his interest.

'Did you know for instance,' I said, 'that a smuggler was thought to be a traitor to his mates on Romney Marsh and that he was beaten to death by them and his body cut to pieces and spread about the marshes?'

The boy moved back from the library's door. His faith in the library had been slightly restored.

'And,' I continued, anxious to build on my success, 'you may be interested in the murder of a Customs Officer by smugglers. The smugglers tied him with an informer to a horse and whipped them - even when the two fell upside down and were also being kicked by the feet of the horse. They buried the Customs Officer alive and committed dreadful barbarities on the other man.'

His attention showed that he greatly approved of the activities of smugglers.

'And that's all in there?' he asked, pointing to the book which, in my anxiety to please, I had forgotten.

'Well no.'

He looked at me as if I had betrayed him.

'But it is in a book.' I hastened on because, as far as I remembered, the book had been written in the 1740s and certainly was not in stock at headquarters. 'But there are plenty of books about smugglers, and pirates.'

'Pirates?'

'Real blackguards some of them.' I was on safer ground here. I knew there was a good children's book on pirates at Hennor Park but my enthusiasm to convert blinded me to the fact that it was not one an eight year old would be able to read.

'What did pirates do?'

'You know what they did,' I answered. 'Made people walk the plank. Murdered whole ships' companies to get at their cargoes.'

'They really did that then. It's not just stories.'

'They really did it.'

He smiled:

'Can you bring 'em down for me?'

'Of course,' I gestured expansively.

He looked to his colleagues and was amazed to see that they were staring not at their leader, but at me. I had made an impact.

Now, all you have to do to join the library is to fill in a form.'

'Me writing's not up to much.'

'That's all right, I'll fill it in for you.'

I took five yellow forms and each of the boys told me his name and address.

'Now all you have to do,' I said, handing the forms out, 'is to get your Mum or your Dad to sign it.'

'Mum or Dad?'

'Yes. To sign it.'

He looked at me as if he expected a trap.

'Why?'

'Well, they... Well it's just the rules.'

I was determined not to mention responsibility for loss or damaged books. This would involve just that element of authority that I wished to avoid.

I continued: 'And if you can't get the books back any time and they bring them for you, we'll know who they are.'

This seemed to satisfy him. He smiled again and led his troop out of the library.

'That's the last you'll see of them,' laughed Jock.

But I was convinced it would not be.

The hour was approaching seven and I began to pack up the books I had to take back to headquarters. Jock was putting the metal gratings onto the bookshelves to protect the books from damage during other functions.

There was a noise outside and then a stream of yellow confetti poured in through the door.

I stooped to look at it while some of the pieces still eddied in the still evening air. But I knew before I did so what I should find. The shredded remains of five yellow membership cards.

Bus Going Nowhere

He had not looked outside for some time. Inside the shelter the rain could be ignored.

Newspapers draped the seats which extended round the three enclosed sides of the shelter - newspapers which had represented bedding to the tramps who had not long left it.

The man in the shelter was aware of his bedraggled appearance; his coat, its collar still protectively raised around his neck, was still wet from the rain which had soaked through his clothing and dampened the enthusiasm with which he had greeted the morning.

Would he sleep in the shelter? Would this be sufficient atonement? He looked up at last and noticed, for the first time since entering the shelter, the dark and threatening sky. Then he began thinking about his day. Why did he feel that he needed to atone? Because the girl had rejected his advances? Was that not a natural thing for a man to do - what he had done. He looked down at the newspaper on the seat.

The headline proclaimed a rape case. Must we broadcast such acts; should we not be quietly ashamed? He had no such reason to be ashamed. He just felt guilty for the moment because he was a man; he bore the guilt for all men.

He recalled his wife, in the agony of childbirth. His fault. It had been his idea to start a family, and she had been the one to suffer. And now, several months after the birth of their son, she continued to reject him. Had rejected him today when he had tried... but he had realised his mistake in time. He had come out with the vague intention of getting on the first bus and going... he didn't know where. He wasn't very sure what to do. He was only sure that his wife no longer loved him and that it was somehow his fault.

The girl was young - about twenty. She came into the shelter looking straight ahead into its gloomy interior. Then she turned. The man turned too, both for the first time aware of each other's presence.

The girl looked out at the prematurely gathering dusk and back, fleetingly, at the man as if making a decision. Her decision seemed to be that the cold wet dark was preferable to his company. She moved back into the oncoming night.

'No! No please! Don't go,' he said.

He was surprised at himself. Why was her presence important? Why was it necessary for her not to shun him - be afraid of him?

She continued, slowly, to walk.

'I'm sorry. Please. You are safe in here with me.'

The girl looked back and stood outside the shelter. Soon the rain beat harder on the building's roof and puddles began to form immediately outside its shelter. She moved back to within a few feet of the shelter's entrance.

The man felt happier.

'I am sorry to frighten you. I'm waiting for a bus.'

'You'll wait a long time. The last bus has gone,' said the girl.

The man expressed surprise. He did not care about buses, but he wanted to reassure the girl. What otherwise would he be doing in a bus shelter unless, like her, he was sheltering from the rain?

He rose from his seat and she backed towards the entrance, watching him closely.

'What are you doing here?' she asked.

It was a difficult question coming as it did from a complete stranger. Should he tell her the whole story? It would be best.

The girl listened with an air of detachment, looking every now and then as if she were willing to walk out at any point if the rain eased.

'Why are you telling me this?' she asked.

He didn't know why. He said so. She leaned against the shelter's wall and, eventually, sat down.

'You see I am no threat to you,' he said.

She looked up. The alarm he had attempted to allay had been aroused.

'But I see you think I am. You are worried by my presence. There is no need. Don't you see I need you to tell me you are not uncomfortable in my presence? I need reassurance.'

He turned to the newspaper flaunting its banner headline obscenely against the edge of the bench.

'We are not all like that. He was a beast.'

The rain showed no sign of easing. The girl sighed. There was nothing to be gained by walking into the blinding rain; she crossed the shelter and sat beside him.

He smiled but there was no reaction from the girl who continued to stare out into the dark as if he were not there.

'You do understand?' he asked pleadingly.

The girl continued to stare.

'Please say you understand.'

This time the girl turned to him, sighed and settled further back into the seat. It was enough. She had relaxed. It was all he wished to know.

For a moment neither spoke; then he asked again:

'Would you trust me to... to?'

She stared, awaiting the finish of his sentence. But he stumbled into silence and looked away.

It was at this moment that she drew the knife from her handbag and plunged it into his body.

She did not look at him again - just picked up the fallen newspaper and, tucking it into her bag, left the shelter.

The rain soaked through her thin coat and the rumbling of distant thunder merged with the noise of the traffic as night began to fall.

Easy When You Know How

It was a hard challenge, but Albert had always relished challenges. He crouched in the hallway; the worst part was over. He had broken in, forced the lock on the front door and even negotiated the mortise on the door of the flat. The chain had been one of those modern ones - built to resist all but the most determined of burglars. But he was the most determined of burglars and he had cut through it. There was nothing now to keep him from his goal.

She had taken his key and assumed that it would keep him out. She had padlocked the windows. Laughable - his cutters would have taken out a portion of glass more easily than she could cut one of her cakes. More easily, he grinned, remembering her cooking. However he had not tried the windows. There were only two external walls with windows, one facing the high street, the other the back yard. In either case she could have seen him coming - and he had his own reasons for not wanting that.

He crouched in the corridor. Only one more barrier. His heart began to beat wildly: he was so near. His step was soundless as he approached the door of the lounge and pressed his ear against it. There were sounds within. He had struck lucky first time. He listened again. She was humming. Albert laughed. She would not be humming in a moment.

He grasped the door knob and turned it gently. Gently. She was still humming; she had heard nothing. He took the knob in both hands, pushed it and turned. There was no squeak; it turned sweetly and the door gently opened to his pressure.

Quietly releasing the handle he looked through the crack in the door. She was going over to the Hi-Fi, placing a record on the turntable. In three quick, soundless strides he was behind her. She turned: he lifted his knife and brought it down. Down… down. Her screams were ringing in his ears. They mixed with his laughter. It was so funny.

He stood over her cowed body.

85

'Did you think you could keep me out you silly little fool?' She shrugged, her fear subsiding.

'You say I'm a lousy burglar. You tell me I couldn't even break into my own home. You take my key and challenge me; you say you are safe from anyone in this flat - that no one could break in. Oh, what a laugh. Well I have shown you my worth. You have never really known it since you married me - always saying how much better other husbands are. And I have shown you something else - how easy it would be for me to murder you if I wished. Not that I would,' he laughed. 'Not now. Not after this.'

She smiled again. She was still smiling as she placed her hand on his; as she pushed the dagger, still in his hand, up under his ribs and into the soft flesh of his body. She registered his look of astonishment. He was so foolish; had fallen for her trick as she knew he would. He could not resist showing what a good burglar he was; she did not want to be married to a burglar.

She had not touched the knife. It had been his hand she forced up into that most vulnerable spot. She need do nothing except push over a few chairs, create the evidence of a struggle...

'Yes officer,' she rehearsed. 'He had become unbearable. I found his key in his jacket and when he went out I locked the Yale on the front door of the building, the mortise and the chain on the flat door. He was a criminal and becoming more violent. He broke in; he crossed all my defences, and then he came at me. Oh God, I had to defend myself; it was terrible I...'

She picked up the 'phone, patted her hair into place and dialled 999.

'Police please,' she said, her voice trembling.

Charlton Church Lane

'*Life Without Women*. It's a book about Solly,' said Mike as the book landed on his table.

'And did you enjoy it, Mr Thomas, sir?'

Dai Thomas looked at Mike.

'I only 'ad it for two minutes didn't I boy? You can't read a book in two minutes.'

'Solly can,' said Stalky, ''cause he gets through the pictures at a real rate an' 'e misses out the words.'

'Can't understand 'em,' said Mike.

'Can't read 'em,' said Stalky.

Solly walked into the room.

Dai Thomas looked at Mike and Stalky. It was a look which suggested that the talk about Solly should cease during his presence.

'*Life Without Women*, Solly. A book about you, look,' repeated Mike.

Solly ignored him and sank into a chair.

'Bleedin' Harley Street. Why do I always get Harley Street?'

'Because it's good for your great fat body to get some exercise, that's why,' answered Mike.

Dai Thomas retreated to his table and lit a cigarette. It was useless to interfere when Mike was bating Solly; it only made him worse. And Dai didn't mind very much anyway. Solly was a moany bastard.

Dai was more interested in studying his pay cheque. 'Seven quid,' he thought, 'how does a man keep a woman and three youngsters on seven quid a week?' Dai was rarely angry but, when he looked across the room at The Student, he felt a pang of envy. He'd been here two minutes filling in before returning to dental college, and he got as much as Dai. Seven pounds - and he probably spent it as he chose. Not on new shoes for the kids...

A voice thundered across the room from a small adjoining

room.

'Kelly.'

Kelly threw down his book in anger muttering: 'Just when I get to a good bit,' and walked out of the room.

Kelly was the second student. It had taken him a week to fit into the pattern, to resent being called out on jobs. For life in the Messengers' Department was largely one of inactivity. Always someone must be on call for an urgent job; usually about four of the staff of seven were just awaiting a call. But after a while even Kelly, a bright student earning some extra money, got used to the inactivity and resented the call to work.

Boss - he was never known by any other name - was big. He supported his men like a champion and treated them like dirt. He had never been seen without a cigarette in his mouth other than when he was actually eating meals and then his first action after he stopped chewing was to light another. As Boss spoke the cigarette in his mouth jogged up and down spilling ash onto the table. Kelly, as usual, watched the accumulating ash waiting for it to fall again.

'Are you bloody listening?'

'Yes.'

'Well bloody look like you're bloody listening.'

Kelly looked as if he was listening.

'You take a taxi.'

'Oh?' said Kelly, eyes raised.

'You take a *taxi*, cretin. The taxi that leaves London Bridge at 10.30. You give the bloody driver 10%.'

'10% of what?'

Boss snarled and threw across a sheet of paper,

'That's the rate per mile in taxi charges. And that,' he said, throwing a map and map measurer, 'is how far it is. Are you capable of working it out?'

For some minutes Kelly ran the tiny wheel of the map measurer down the roads leading to his destination. Next he checked the taxi charges.

'Five pounds?'

'Five pounds, eight and ten pence.'

'But how...?'

'Did I get it so exact? Don't be bloody soft. You're supposed to be one of the intelligent ones. Have you ever heard of a taxi driver charging five pounds exactly?'

Kelly never travelled by taxi and he suspected that Boss never did either, but it seemed to make sense.

'So I go by train and claim the taxi fare?'

Boss threw up his hands in mock astonishment.

'You *are* intelligent. You cotton on to things like bloody Einstein. Get out. And split the difference between the train and taxi fare. I know what it is; don't try to fiddle me.'

'I wouldn't.'

Boss laughed: 'No, I know.'

On his way out Kelly Murphy cringed as Boss bellowed 'Mike' across his shoulders. Kelly passed Mike Murphy as the spindly lad walked into the office.

'Now, Mike. Ludgate Circus.'

'Bus?' said Mike.

'Bleedin' walk,' said Boss, 'do you think they're soft in the head? Claim bus for that and we'll be asking a fare to go up in the lift. Hang on.' The 'phone had rung.

'Where?' said Boss into the 'phone. 'Charlton? That's not a place it's a bloody football team. Yes... yes. Oh Christ, Sam, if the girl can go can't she take the package?' Boss grinned. 'No, you're right, Sam, we don't want clerical staff taking over messenger jobs. Murphy will go. Yes, of course he's reliable. He just looks stupid.'

Mike grinned: 'I don't even look stupid.'

Boss ignored the remark: 'You've gotta go to Chariton Church Lane to deliver a package.'

'What about Ludgate Circus?'

'It'll still be there when you get back.'

'How do I go to Charlton. Taxi?'

'No can do this time, you'll have to rough it on bleedin' Southern Region. You've got company.'

'Who?'

'A bird'

'A very old bird?'

'Miss Green.'

'Christ,' Mike said.

Mike waited at the bottom of the steps which led to an imposing marble entrance facade. He was twenty one, and taller than his body had expected. Hence his strange appearance. Mike regaled his workmates with stories of his exploits with the opposite sex but it is doubtful whether they were believed; there seemed little likelihood of their being true.

Mike swung round.

'Excuse me. Are you Mr Murphy?'

Mike nodded. The surprise at being so correctly addressed was nothing to the astonishment he felt at looking at the source of the enquiry.

'Miss Green?'

'Miss Avril Green. You were expecting another Miss Green?'

'Yes, Haggy Green... er... Miss... the other Miss Green.'

The girl laughed.

'Haggy Green, yes that sums her up.'

Mike was walking towards the bus stop. The girl was young, was wearing a white blouse and grey skirt. Mike noticed the way her pert breasts bobbed as she walked. Not at all what he had expected.

In his dreams Mike would not simply have sat next to this girl, trying not to catch her eye, trying not to look down at her legs. In the stories he told she would by now have been putty in his hands, the willing victim of his romantic patter.

'Have you worked here long?'

Mike nodded. He'd worked at Handel House since leaving school.

'And what do you hope to do?'

Mike looked puzzled. He didn't hope to do anything.

'No secret ambitions?'

Mike shook his head.

They lapsed into silence. He felt he ought to say something but what does one say to a girl like that?

'You've... er... got to go to Charlton Church Lane?'

'Yes,' the girl replied. She had.

'You be staying long?'

'Oh about ten minutes. It's only a few reports a consultant has for us. Mr Armitage wants me to look at them.'

'Then I'd best wait for you.'

'Yes, it would be nice to have company back.'

Mike grinned. The prospect of the return journey with the girl filled him with intense pleasure - a strange emotion since the present journey made him feel awkward and ill at ease.

The girl inhaled deeply, and stretched. Her breasts pressed firmly against her blouse. She must have realised that Mike was staring in amazed admiration.

She lowered her arms and smiled.

'London Bridge,' she said. Mike looked at her stupidly.

'We'd better get off.' 'Oh yes,' he said.

The train made its way through the South East London suburbs. Maze Hill. Westcombe Park. Charlton, and their errand was quickly completed.

The sun had penetrated the morning mist by the time Mike and Miss Green returned to the station. Children were playing in front of the post office outside the station. Mike idly wondered why they were not at school. As Mike sat on the train seat he could feel Miss Green's body pressed against him. For once he was glad of the restricting double seats on Southern Region's suburban services.

He engineered small movements, checking his ticket, looking at his watch so that his arm would move against her side. Then he held out her ticket on the palm of his hand.

'You had better take yours.' There was no need for her to take hers. He had presented the return tickets on the outward journey; he could have done so on the return. It had made him feel connected to her, and he had hoped people would assume they were married or...

But in holding out the ticket he intended that she should have to lean over him, touch his hand.

She took the ticket and settled back in her seat.

It was the gloves that puzzled Mike. Why should she wear gloves on such a day? He picked them up as she left the bus and hastily put them into his pocket.

It was too much of a coincidence that she should wear the gloves - and leave them on the bus. Mike smiled. They had been left deliberately. She wanted him to take them back to her, to make a date.

Mike walked proudly beside her. Why could he not make a date now? Was he scared of a refusal when she had given him the sign? No, she realised he was shy under that self-confident exterior. She knew it would take time and she had given it to him.

Mike lit a cigarette and leaned back in his seat so that its back rested against the wall behind him.

'So she was that nice, Mike?' asked Dai Thomas.

'Like putty in me 'ands too.' Mike inhaled deeply. 'Pert little tits, curvy frame, and did you notice the legs?'

'Never seen 'er, Mike, but I can imagine them.'

Mike smiled.

'Pity you ain't gonna see her again, isn't it, Mike?' said Kelly.

Mike smiled again. But the booming voice of Boss summoned him. 'Ludgate bleedin' Circus. Forgotten?'

Mike had forgotten. It didn't matter. He had all day. All week. He strolled towards the exit leaving Kelly grinning behind him.

'So little Miss Green was a bit of alright?'

'Never seen 'er boyo,' said Dai, 'sounds like it don't it?'

Stalky was less sure: 'It's all in his mind. The only Miss Green I know is built like a pelican.'

'Wrong one boy. 'E told me about her - he was expecting her see?'

When Mike returned only Solly remained, drinking tea from a plastic cup. Mike slapped him on the back so that the tea slopped over. Solly didn't look up. He put down the cup and got a cloth. 'Bleedin' jerk,' he said.

'Well, Solly, who will it be tonight. Sophia Loren or Bridget Bardot?'

'Piss off.'

'Well I like that. Here's me offerin' you the pick...'

'Piss off.'

Mike grinned

'Where we been today then?'

'Harley Street.'

'I know you've been to Harley Street, we all heard about that.

Haven't you been anywhere else?'

Solly hadn't.

'Oh dear that's not enough exercise. Or do you spend your nights leaping from one bird to another?' Solly started to drink his tea.

The gloves were burning a hole in Mike's pocket. He had to take them up before she left for lunch. Later would not do. Anything could happen. She could go sick, have to go out for a long period...

As he stepped into the lift doubts were beginning to assail him.

Kelly pushed the lift lever forward and the gates clanged behind him. 'Where to?'

'Seven.'

Kelly smiled. 'Seven?'

'Yes seven. Quality Control,' he said firmly.

'Do you want to tell us about it?'

Mike's bravado had gone. He didn't want to talk about it.

Miss Green's office was one of those which had been converted to open plan. Mike had never been inside it before and the lack of privacy concerned him. He saw her working at the far end. He would have to walk past all those eyes. She looked up as he approached the desk. And smiled.

He kept his hands on the gloves in his pocket.

'Er, Miss Green.'

Miss Green could not keep up her smile for much longer.

'Your gloves.'

'Oh,' her hand flew to her mouth.

'I've er... I've got them. On the bus you...'

She took them from him, leaned over the desk and gave him a peck of a kiss on the cheek.

'Oh you lovely boy. Thanks.' She took them and placed them in her drawer.

'I was wondering... er... if,' said Mike.

She was waiting.

'If you... er... realised you'd left them.'

Miss Green hadn't realised. She thanked him again.

Mike stood at the desk as if transfixed.

'Bye,' he said.

'Bye,' she smiled.

Kelly was waiting with the lift door open. He stood aside to let Mike in.

'How'd it go?'

Mike didn't reply.

'I've been hearing about your Miss Green,' persisted Kelly. 'Seems she's well sought after. You've done well there,' Kelly grinned. 'You *have* done well there haven't you?'

Mike turned.

'Shut up. Just shut your bloody mouth.'

'Mm, you haven't done at all well have you? Well perhaps it's just as well. She seems to have some funny habits.'

'Funny habits?'

'Yes, she lives with Murdoch in Accounts for one. That's a funny habit isn't it?'

Mike closed his mouth which had fallen open.

'Oh, and she wears gloves - black ones wherever she goes. Strange that. Did you find out any more about her?'

'Yes she's bleedin' forgetful.'

'Ha,' said Kelly. 'She'd forgotten who you were since this morning had she?' Kelly laughed loudly. 'Do you want to get out, Mike, we're at the ground floor. Or do you want to stay here all day and confide in me?'

Mike walked out of the lift without answering. Instead of turning towards the Messengers' Room, he walked to the exit. He could hear Boss's booming voice calling: 'Where the bleedin' 'ell is that bugger Murphy?' Mike continued to walk down the steps that led to the building. At the bottom he sat on a concrete plinth. Traffic passed and pedestrians pushed by him. Fellow employees hurried past him up the steps. He stared out on the passing scene. But he saw nothing.

Child of the Man

He sat back. At last the working day was over. His child played on the floor and for a moment he watched him. Watched his clumsy attempts to fit the cups of the children's toy into each other.

He smiled and knelt beside the child, placing one cup inside the other as the manufacturer had intended. The child was too young but it was amusing to watch as it took the cups again, spurred on by having seen the apparently insoluble problem solved before its eyes.

The child's father retired to his chair and watched as the child stared at the cups again, intense in its concentration. The cups came together; the rim of one slid on the base of the other and fell out of the child's grasp. At last the effort was too much; it began to bang the cups together, perhaps partly because of frustration. Perhaps partly because this was something he understood. Something he could do. And it made a pleasing noise.

To his father it was not so pleasing. He took the cups from the child and placed them on a table out of reach. At first the child looked up in disappointment, about to cry. Then the cups were substituted with a toy. The cups were forgotten. The child's large eyes filled with laughter. He gurgled, communicated with the universal language of a child and hugged the toy to him.

For some time the child and the father sat content. Then, as his son was taken to his cot, the man picked up a newspaper and began to read. The news was bad; it was always bad. Without the child, he felt alone in a world from which he would willingly take refuge in the simplicity of his son's.

He opened a window and watched as the resulting draught of air flapped the net curtain against the window frame. He reached for his brief case, took out a file of papers and began to work. The clock ticked loudly on the mantel piece. It was eight o'clock. He lit his pipe, sat back enjoying the sensation of the smoke in his mouth. Then he returned to his work.

For three hours he continued to work while his wife knitted. At times he merely watched the needles flash up and down, the dexterous movements of her hands appearing to have no connection with the woman who drove them. At times she even read from a magazine. He returned to his work. His work could not be mechanically performed, nor would it produce a useful end product such as the garment which grew, perceptively, on his wife's lap. He watched as she closed the window and left the room. He too must go to bed.

Before entering the bedroom he permitted himself one last look at his infant. He thought that the child's eyes were open, staring, but they could not have been for the steady, heavy rhythm of its breath indicated that it was asleep. Then the man saw something that arrested his attention. The cups with which his child had been playing stood on the table beside his cot. They were neatly fixed inside one another. His father had seen his wife carry them into the child's room and place them, separately, on the same table. Again he looked at the child. Again he had the uncomfortable sensation that the child was aware of his presence, was watching him. But no, the eyes were not fixed on him, however they were, without question, open. Quietly the man, with one last look at the cups, closed the door and retired, uneasily, to bed.

The noises in the night could be ignored. Even in a new house there were noises. New wood creaked; windows rattled. Only a particularly sensitive man would have listened to the steady, small footsteps and been afraid. For they could not have been footsteps; they were house noises.

In the morning the man looked in at his child, who slept, still, in his cot. Nothing in the room had moved although the door seemed wider open than he had left it on the previous evening.

He descended the stairs and boiled a kettle of water. At seven o'clock he heard his child cry. It was a normal sound and he welcomed it. He poured the water into the tea pot and smiled; it was good to have a son.

The sun was strong, the day inviting. He poured milk into two cups and took out cereal bowls. His wife could be heard moving, roused by the cries of her child. A primitive instinct — to succour, to protect. His future was in his child and its future was his yearning for eternity.

He drew the lounge curtains, placing the breakfast crockery on the table. His case had been packed methodically the day before. A mechanical process; he could not remember doing it. His car awaited him; the 7.55. train awaited him. The timetable was fixed. One deviation from it would disturb his day, his week.

He sat with a cup of tea, allowing the cool morning to disturb his neatly combed hair; watching fellow early risers open their garage doors and their cars disappear into the endless ritual procession on the A22. Life had been good. He supposed it still was.

His child was now quiet; it had been fed, satisfied. It would be smiling, playing with his wife's necklace. He lay down his cup and mounted the stairs.

The day was done. The garage door slammed and the man's wife collected up the toys strewn around the floor. 'Daddy will be cross.' Daddy would not have been cross. Daddy would have been delighted that his son had been enjoying himself. 'But Daddy would be tired. Daddy is cross when he is tired.'

The front door yielded to a push; she always released the lock at five to seven knowing that he would soon be home. If his train were late it didn't matter. The dinner would not get cold.

He sat down; placed his brief case down on his lap, unzipped it, and took out his pipe.

'I started a bank account today. For the child.'

She smiled.

'I thought about the firm; perhaps a junior partner?'

'But he is so young. Why do we have to....?'

'Because we have to live. Because he will not start on the shop floor. Preparations have to be made when he is young.'

The child gurgled, threw a plastic brick into a trolley and crawled to the trolley, supporting himself on its handle.

'He will be walking soon.'

She smiled. Yes he would.

He took some work out of his brief case, put it down beside him. Then, in irritation, he lit his pipe and watched his child. The work could wait. The child was tired. He should already be in bed. He was always kept up until seven fifteen.

'It is too late,' his wife said.

'It is too late but I see my child.'

'You see him at his worst. He is tired and...'

'But I see him.'

The child was carried to bed, a meal dispensed with, and work resumed. He watched the flashing needles, was dimly aware of the television screen, constantly changing its brightness. The papers lay on his lap, a pen in his hand. Very little work was done but his attention was constantly drawn back to it. His son would be greater than he. He would start higher. And with hard work...

He looked into his son's room. He had grown used to the uncomfortable feeling that the child's eyes were open, staring. What astonished him was the boy's arm. As he watched, it rose from the side of the boy's body and clasped the side of the cot. He turned on the light; the movement had been so alarming, unnatural. The hand released the side of the cot, the arm fell back and the child appeared still to be asleep. He moved to the side of the cot, made one or two unnecessary adjustments to the bed clothes and stroked the child's cheek. It slept on.

His wife was standing beside him. She smiled. He smiled. He told her nothing of his fears. Already he felt them to be groundless. Why should not a child grasp the side of its cot in its sleep?

But the fear remained with him. As he tried to sleep, the noises of the house took possession of him; the creaking of the wardrobe beat a steady tattoo in his heart; the rhythmic flutter of the net curtain stirred his breath; the steady, steady beat of... He listened. His heartbeats were loud. But louder was the steady, mechanical step. Louder than his heartbeat but softer than the natural noises of the night. They continued - those tiny steps.

He did not go into the corridor fearing what he might see. Then he heard a sound as of a gate being unlatched. What gates were there in the house? Then he realised. The gate to stop his child falling down the stairs; the gate his child was now opening with the ease of an adult.

No, he was dreaming; not dreaming perhaps but dozing. His child meant so much to him. He was working too hard and it was having its effect - making him have unnecessary fears for his child. He turned out the bedside lamp. His wife was already asleep. It was not his child that was taking those mechanical regular steps; it was not his child who had unlatched the safety gate. It was not his child who was taking those small regular steps down the stairs. It was not his child.

The sun was shining brightly. He pulled back the curtains. It would be another bright day. It would brighten his drive to the station although it would intensify the discomfort of his train journey. He dressed quietly. Then he walked out onto the landing. The first thing that met his eye was the safety gate. It was swinging loose. It had been unlatched. He rushed to his child's room; it was alright. The child was lying much as it had been left the night before. He stepped through the safety gate, latched it and descended the stairs.

The bright day continued into the mellow light of evening. The air, at last, was cool and there were long shadows into which to retreat. The man settled into his chair and fumbled with a parcel. 'You have got a toy for the child?'

He opened the packet and withdrew a bolt.

'A bolt for the safety gate?' She laughed quietly. Then laughter took control of her. He could hear her in the kitchen and her laughter mixed with the ringing of pots and pans and the sound of the gas jets.

He lay awake. There could be no sleep while those footsteps took their measured tread. The latch was tried. He became more alert. Then came the sound that he had dreaded, the sound of a bolt being drawn and a gate opened. He sat up in bed. The child was descending the stairs. He accepted it now. He accepted that a child who could not walk, who could not fathom the simplest educational toy, who had not yet reached his first birthday - could be the same child who every night...

He leapt from the bed and rushed to the landing. He looked down apprehensively. He could see a small figure turning the bend at the bottom of the stairs. He followed.

Every movement of the child was performed mechanically but with ease. The way it turned the key in the lock of the bureau; unzipped the brief case and looked through the papers inside. It was uncanny - as if the child understood them; as if on reading them he rejected them, throwing them down with a sigh, then replacing them in the brief case. The child looked around the room and then, with another sigh, mounted the stairs again. In the morning it would be found asleep. His wife would feed him. He would chuckle, fumble with his educational toys.

Every night he heard it. There seemed no way but the way he chose. He would follow the child and put him back in his cot. Then, after a while, the steady step would be heard again and he would follow again. There must be a night when he would fall asleep, be unable to follow the child...

He slept.

The alarum rang at his bedside. He rolled over, turned it off, and sleepily rubbed his eyes. He had never needed to turn off the alarum before, but he had never before been so in need of sleep. People had begun to notice. His work had suffered. He had even fallen asleep at his desk. He looked at his wife but did not disturb her. The child would soon cry. That would disturb her.

He descended the stairs, fastening the safety gate behind him. He filled the electric kettle with water and placed the cups on the work surface. He waited for his child to cry. It was seven o'clock.

He replaced the dishes and saucepans from the draining board in the cupboard.

While he waited for the kettle to boil he took out his pipe and filled it with tobacco.

He made the tea and poured it. There was still no sound of movement from the bedroom and the child had still not awoken.

He went into the lounge. His brief case was not at the side of the settee where he expected to find it. God! This tiredness. He was losing his routine. He always packed his briefcase, left it by the side of the settee ready for the morning.

He sighed and went back into the kitchen. He would take the tea upstairs, give it to his wife. He sat on the bed and drank his own.

'The child should be awake,' he said.

His wife yawned and nodded.

He replaced his tea cup on the bedside cabinet and went into the child's room. The cot was empty.

He rushed to the cot. The cover had been folded back and the child was gone. He ran to the top of the stairs, cursed the vigilance which had made him fix the bolt on the safety gate and ran down the stairs. He searched the lounge, the dining room, the toilet, the cupboards. His wife was calling from the landing.

What was the matter?

He rushed up the stairs, two at a time. In a frenzy he searched every room. He heard his wife scream as she discovered the empty cot. He shouted comforting phrases which she could not hear above the sound of her own voice.

'Soon find him. Don't know what's happened. Soon be alright.'

He joined his wife in the child's room. She was sitting by the cot crying.

'Something terrible has happened.'

He ignored her, looked under the cot, and into the child's clothes cupboard which he knew was too small for the child to squeeze into.

Then he looked out of the window. Down to the garden below where the tiny body of his son lay.

The Very Average Ebury Smith

Ebury fiddled with the lights. The cine lights screwed into a tripod unlike the recommended arc lights. But they would have to do. Ebury held the screw again. He wished he did not always have the same uncomfortable sensation when he thought of the word 'screw'. She would be here soon and he must not blush like a schoolboy every time a double meaning occurred to him.

Ebury had taken up photography because it had appealed to his sense of glamour. Not entirely, he thought, because the word photography conjured up for him the idea of centre spreads and glamour pictures. Not entirely, but that was a serious consideration when he purchased equipment on hire-purchase that, on reflection, he could not afford.

He had an artistic flair, an artistic temperament and an artistic blindness to reality. He was presentable without being handsome, witty without being highly intelligent and, in all things, incurably average. Photography might cure that, he thought. Photography might raise him above his unambitious equals, the men in the street, the stuff of whom future obscurity is made.

Ebury had no intention of being a statistic in social history, although he had no plan, other of course than the attic and the camera and the cine lights, by which to reach a position which might qualify him for a place in the minutiae of history. He would be satisfied with a mention in an obscure thesis - few people of any eminence at all can have escaped the scholar in search of totally unresearched material - but he insisted (in his face to face with the Fates) that he must be named. He did not wish to appear as a road statistic or as a victim of a certain disease or as a member of an age group, sex group... although he was prepared to admit, with unusually perceptive honesty, that this might be a lesser role he would be called upon to play.

Only Ebury's name singled him out as unusual. One would

have thought that his parents would have anticipated his future aver-age-ness and supplied him with a Christian name like John to go with his acceptably average surname of Smith. However they had acted on an impulse and decided upon Ebury. Ebury himself admitted that they may have had a reason but, if so, he was unaware of it.

Ebury squatted behind his camera. He had tried writing - in fact writing had been his first choice - but presumably every agent, pub-lisher and editor had thrown aside his work with the condemnatory cry of: 'Average. Bloody average'. He had tried sport. He had beaten people at golf, tennis, table tennis, cycling... the list was endless. But they were the weaker of the world's competitors. He had never attained the glam-our of mention in the local press; his victories had gone unrecorded, his defeats unlamented.

He threaded the film into the take up spool, pressed the per-forations onto the cog and snapped the back of the camera shut. The air of finality was symbolical. The lady who was to perch in front of his camera would grace the covers of periodicals of international repute or he, Ebury Smith, would... He did not want to think further than the delicious thought of fame. 'Taken by Ebury Smith on Ektachrome 200. Yashica FR f1.4'; 'Taken by Ebury Smith on Fuji RIOO. Nikon FE f1.4'; 'Taken by Ebury Smith on Agfacolor...' There was a ring at the door. The dreams evaporated. The newly acquired camera receded into the background as he looked at his single SLR. It was going to be another balls up. She would be ugly, with no dress sense, impossible make-up, no grace; the film would jam; the bulbs would go; the... The summons from the front door became more imperative.

He descended the stairs with a feeling of impending doom and flung open the door.

At first he thought the agency must have made a mistake and sent him a man. Then he realised that the man was a postman and that he was proffering a little orange box.

Ebury held out his hand.

'Holiday snaps is they?' chatted the postman.

'Snaps!' shrieked Ebury, nettled.

'Well they looks like snaps. Them boxes...'

'Hold photographs, slides, but not snaps! I am a photographer. I own a camera not a pin-hole.'

'Oh,' said the postman. 'Better than mine then?'

'No doubt.'

'I have a...'

'I'm not really interested in your hobbies. I am a professional man and...'

'... a Hasselblad,' the Postman continued.

Ebury gulped.

'A Hasselblad?' he said weakly.

'Yes. You'd be having somethin' more pricey, 500 lenses, starbursts, sound cine...'

Ebury gulped again.

'Quite,' he said. Now I really must curtail this interesting conversation. I am expecting my model.'

'Oh, blimey. Blonde bird is it, million dollars and a bit more, dress like it was covering up the wrong bits, voice like music, walk like a flamingo, body like a nymph...?'

The man had to be stopped. The performance was very likely continuous, Ebury thought:

'Why do you say...?' Ebury croaked.

'Oh, she's headin' this way. Arst for yer number. I showed 'er where it was.'

'So why, I wonder, is she not here yet?' His croak now made his speech barely intelligible. The postman must have caught the gist for he replied:

'Oh you know what them birds have to do before a session. Grease their pubes and such like.'

This was too much for Ebury. He slammed the door, mounted the stairs two at a time and launched himself into the attic slamming the trap door shut behind him. It was one thing to lust after women; it was one thing to crave a sight of naked voluptuous curves. It was one thing to view the displayed charms of an epitome of female beauty. It was quite another to encounter such a paragon in the flesh. Ebury gulped at the word flesh. The phrase 'grease their pubes' was still rushing round his head seeking an exit and banging about in his brain in an effort to get out.

Ebury took a hold of his galloping emotions. He must sit quietly. She would be here in a moment and she must not find a quivering mass of inarticulate humanity, incapable of a relatively simple exercise like pointing a camera and pressing the shutter. He felt a little better. He was beginning to accept that the postman had been exaggerating. He began to wonder whether, indeed, the postman had been joking. Making fun of him. Holding up his pomposity to ridicule. Ebury felt rather guilty at the recollection of his attitude towards a man who owned a Hasselblad. Or said he owned a Hasselblad. Why must he always believe people?

The most logical answer was that this man owned an Instamatic which he rarely used because he found it too complicated. He had seen a hideous hag at the end of the street asking directions to the house of the notoriously average Ebury Smith and had hit upon the obvious idea of having some fun at the expense of the said Smith.

He felt better. His breathing was returning to a more normal rate. He exhaled. Why was he so gullible? Of course the model was a Medusa in human form; she would be suitably ugly, lack dress-sense, sport impossible make-up, and be devoid of grace. The film would definitely jam; the bulbs give up the ghost early in the proceedings; the... Yes, he was reassured by the normality of it all. One of the photos would be purchased by her Auntie Laura who would complain about the price. Another would be praised by her Uncle Len who would say that it captured her perfectly, which would mean that no one in their right mind would buy it... The front door bell rang.

He made his way composedly down the stairs... It was probably a hawker or a schoolboy wanting his ball back or a lady asking whether he had seen her budgie or... The postman had been right. The creature's arm shot out to support Ebury Smith as he slumped against the door frame.

'Ebury Smith?' she queried.

'Argh.'

'I beg your pardon?'

'I said errgh.'

The creature smiled and, assuming that he was new to the country and struggling to conquer the complexities of its language, walked past him into the hallway.

She looked back. The poor man was obviously suffering under some form of physical handicap. He seemed to need support for his every movement. He had finally missed catching the banister rail and deposited himself in a crumpled heap. Poor man. The girl's heart went out to him. To labour under so many difficulties and yet struggle to live a normal life.

'Normal?' he croaked.

The girl apologised. She must have spoken aloud. It was obviously a sore point.

He clearly wished to appear normal.

She took his arm and propelled him up the stairs and into the attic where, as if by instinct, she divined that the session was to be held.

Ebury Smith was struggling to effect some form of calm.

'Right,' he said in what he felt should have been an authoritative manner.

The girl smiled understandingly as if he were a schoolboy smoking his first cigarette. She would have to humour him. It could not be easy labouring under so many handicaps.

Ebury tried to master his hands so that they displayed some sort of co-ordination with the rest of his body. He nonchalantly (or he attempted to make the action nonchalant) moved the angle of the cine lights which he had previously adjusted perfectly to spotlight the place where he anticipated the model would be.

He cursed under his breath as the light spilled over the floor a few yards to the left of the lamps so that the model and her props were plunged into near darkness.

The girl approached him, moved the lights and adjusted their angle to coincide exactly with the ideal subject point at which he himself had arrived previous to her arrival.

'Figh,' he said.

'Pardon?'

'Fine,' he said. Or something like it.

He squatted behind his camera.

'How would you like me?' she asked.

Ebury Smith just stared. It was a question that could be answered in so many ways.

'Theg,' he said pointing madly.

The model moved to the most suitable place for the first photo to be taken and composed herself for the picture.

'One for starters then,' she said smiling.

Ebury crouched before his camera but it was some time before he could locate his model. When an arm came into view he depressed the shutter hoping that at least part of her body would appear on the picture.

'Now,' she said, as if expressing satisfaction with his technique, 'I have my wardrobe or, if you like, I can pose nude.'

'With your wardrobe,' he said, at last vaguely intelligible. He was not ready for nude poses. Barely ready for taking any pictures at all of this delectable creature.

She smiled and disappeared behind the screen, unclipping a small case which apparently held her 'wardrobe'.

When she reappeared it was to a cameraman slowly recovering his cool. The outfit did nothing to discomfit him and pubes, greased or otherwise, did not appear to figure in her plans.

He sank behind his camera, longing for the protection of a black cloth with which the photographers of yesteryear hid their confusion. She looked good. Cool, elegant. There was nothing to do but take the picture.

It was the first of many. In all of them he considered she would appear reasonably near the centre of the composition. If she did not he would put it down to technique. 'That's how you take pictures with a Brownie,' he heard himself say, 'central images and all that. But it is not how you take pictures with a proper camera.'

The session neared its end. He felt reasonably certain that the pictures would be a success. Then it all happened. She had disappeared behind the screen for the last time and all seemed to be over. Until he tripped over the lead from the cine light. Until he thudded against the screen. Until the screen buckled in the middle and sent his model crashing to the floor, her naked body sprawling against a confusing pattern of falling lights and flailing bodies.

Ebury stood up slowly. Would nothing discomfit this glorious paragon? She stood, calmly, and eyed him strangely. Then she smiled:

'Are you sure you don't want one of me - like this?'

Ebury was not sure that he did. He was anxiously looking at the fallen equipment, more in embarrassment at the beautiful naked body in front of him than in concern over possible breakages. He nodded. It was the only possible way he could salvage something memorable from this session. He picked up the light, rescued the camera, and restored it to its precarious perch on the tripod.

Quickly he nodded. He had done it now. There was no turning back. She moved her body to the rhythm of his constantly clicking shutter. She smiled, looked sultry, pouted, assumed erotic poses; grovelled, laughed aloud and shook her head so that her hair cascaded in a golden shower of electronically controlled sunshine.

He was happy. For the first time in months he had succeeded. It remained only to see the results. He bustled her out of the house thanking her profusely. She had been wonderful, superb, exotic, erotic, appealing, revealing... The model marvelled at his sudden controlled language but felt almost reassured as, on her departure, she heard his body crash against the closed front door and fall to an insensible heap on the floor.

It was almost two weeks before Ebury Smith was able to review the results of the session and the time lapse had conquered his optimism and assured him that, despite the efforts of his model, the photographic world was not the one which would welcome him amongst its elite.

His hands were shaking as he entered the shop. He exchanged his money for a wallet of pictures with a feeling of dread. He would start at the end. There was no use in depressing himself by re-living his early failures. He groped to the back of the packet trying to avoid looking at the top of the first picture which exhibited a lot of his attic but very little of his model.

He smiled. It was not so bad. The girl stared back at him. Her image was reasonably sharp, reasonably central and almost perfectly illuminated. It was a good picture. He fished out the penultimate picture. Again good. OK. Then the next. Then the next. Then he sighed. Yes they were good, fairly good, but they were nothing special. His mouth formed the word. Average. Curse it, they were average. They were not bad but, given the girl and the luck, they were pictures that anyone without incurable camera shake and total lack of artistic awareness could have taken. He felt tears start to his eyes, wiped them away and peered more intently, as if it was intensity of observation and not feeling which had caused the dampness in his eyes. The retailer was still staring at him. When Ebury looked up he was astonished to see that the man was smiling - broadly. How dare he? How dare he mock him? He must process pictures for idiots; people who took snaps of cats without heads, fathers without feet, parties without definition, coal holes without flash... Why should he mock him? Why should he laugh at the average Ebury Smith?

But there was something about the smile which held no suggestion of mockery - more... admiration. The impression was confirmed when the smile creased still further and the man said:

'Great!'

'Great?'

'Superb!'

'Superb?'

The retailer discounted the obvious modesty of his client's response.

'Having taken that... that... picture, he looks at the try-outs first. Amazing,' said the shopkeeper. 'I have to hand it to you. Incredible.'

Ebury's thumbing through the pictures became frenetic. Where was it? Which picture among the 'try-outs' had turned out so well?

The girl flashed before him in her many guises: seductress, innocent, nymph... What the hell was this? How did he take...

Then he realised. Had he taken this? A picture of the girl with hair, slightly blurred, breasts swinging in perfect rhythm, eyes turned up to face the camera in wonder, legs held slightly apart... Could his hand really have fallen upon the shutter release as the girl's body had hurtled towards him in a cascade of falling light?

'Superb,' said the man again.

'Not bad' said Ebury.

'Perfect,' said the man.

'Quite nice,' said Ebury.

'Unbeatable,' said the man.

'Yes,' said Ebury.

The Essential Rosie

We never recovered from the day Rosie made love to the driver in a mobile library; he was fifty, she was nineteen but the difference in ages mattered less than the mellowing influence of literature and the exciting thought that she was thrusting two fingers in the face of convention.

She had come to work at the County Library a year before Norman the driver and, in that year, had succeeded in convincing ageing male virgins that the female sex had suffered irreparable loss by their earlier chastity; and the matronly element amongst the staff that she had been born eighteen years too soon.

Not that there were many matronly librarians at HQ, neither were there any hawk-nosed dragons with spectacles. Mostly they were pleasant, in a few cases pretty, in one case beautiful.

I followed Norman.

I suppose the origin of our relationship would seem strange to anyone unaware of Rosie's talent for turning the prosaic into perfect beauty. We met in a broom cupboard on the third day of her employment with the County Library.

But that was before most of the library hierarchy from Chief Librarian to cleaner had succumbed to her charms. During this wholesale de-flowering I lingered somewhere on the fringe, wondering with a mixture of dread and excitement whether I should be next. I was a shy youth and, if my duties as the deliverer of internal mail did not entitle me to a place on one of the higher echelons of the library establishment, I was conscious of a higher social standing than some of her recent victims.

But I was shy. Perhaps that was why she left me to last. Perhaps I was the only one who would follow where Norman the mobile library driver had left off.

Rosie was blonde, petite and quiet. Quiet that is until you felt in the mood for action when she was about as quiet as an A.R.P. thunderflash. She had this way of walking about the building as if preoccu-pied with her own affairs. Then she'd look up and see you and it was as if you'd made her day. Well one day she looked up and did more than smile and pass the time of day. She took hold of my hand and with a proprietary air took me off to her den in the Mobile Library Exchange book store. As I was swept along, my hand nestling happily in hers, I saw the book stacks as ethereal beings, smiling benignly. The out trays from which I normally collected flew past me for all the world like cher-ubims and seraphims dancing attendance upon my fate.

Her den was hidden deep in the bowels of the building and no one witnessed our rush there-ward. All at once and far too soon my hand was released and a place prepared for me.

Rosie pulled up a chair.

'I'm worried about the courier,' she said.

The way she said it the courier service, hitherto the bane of my life, sounded like an exciting new world. I stared. Had I done something wrong?

'No, no,' she cooed resting her hand on mine and stroking it soothingly, 'you have done nothing wrong.'

She made it sound as if I were incapable of error and continued to stroke my hand long after I had been reassured by her smile. Then what had I done?

'Oh my dear Charlie, nothing. I simply wish to know the couri-er timetable. You know I'm so useless at remembering these things and you must help me. I wonder - would you - would you mind very much writing down the last collection times for the different destinations?'

I smiled. It was something I could do without referring to my lists - I knew the times so well. I smiled and took the piece of paper she proffered. Then - it all went. I could not for the life of me remember one time or even one destination. I looked at her helplessly.

'Oh, I *know*,' she said, 'it's absolutely impossible to remember. I don't know how you know where to send everything let alone when. But you just get the list and photocopy it. That will give me another excuse to entertain you in my den for I am so enjoying this visit. Now, just before you go, would you very much mind doing something for me? It's very embarrassing really - I have this feeling there's something on my leg - at the back you know and - well - you don't like to ask *anybody* to help you over things like that do you?'

With this she pulled up her tight skirt and I was presented with the sight of her shapely legs and the tantalising glimpse of the lowermost part of her panties.

'Can you see anything?'

I looked more carefully, concentrating on the job in hand. After an exhaustive search I discovered a long splinter of which just a small portion had entered her skin. I informed her blushingly.

'That's it. Oh that's *it*. That's just where it's sore. Would you mind very much?'

Would I mind?

'Yes would you mind just removing it? I could never do it myself - it's in such an awkward place.'

I gulped.

'Of course if you haven't time?'

I had time. I told her I had time.

I slipped my hand up her skirt, in at the waist band of her tights, over that most delicious bottom and down to the splinter, pulling the tights down with my left hand.

The job was done far too quickly. Stupidly I pulled her tights back up to her waist as if she were incapable of performing the act and held the splinter like a trophy.

'Oh that is it,' she cried. 'Oh I really must.' She kissed me. It had happened too quickly. I had not had time to take it in. But she had kissed me:

'Now, you will bring that list to me won't you?'

'List?'

'Courier times.'

'Courier times,' I repeated woodenly, and then more sensibly. 'Oh yes courier times.'

'Tomorrow?'

'Tomorrow,' I confirmed.

And with that I returned to my room. 'Tomorrow,' I said.

Tomorrow eventually came after an eternity of today. And when it did I was required to perform my normal duties as if it was no special day, as if I did not have a date with destiny.

On the completion of my morning's routine, I took down the courier list and photocopied it. By this time my hands were beginning to tremble and my legs took on the consistency of blancmange - a feeling which rendered movement difficult and purposeful movement impossible.

I did, however, successfully negotiate the stairs to the book store where Rosie was busying herself with some last minute jobs before packing up for lunch. She seemed surprised by my entrance, almost as if she were not expecting me.

I mumbled that I had brought the courier list.

'The courier...?'

'The courier list. Times. You asked for them.'

'Of course I did. Do you know I think I'd forget my head...?'

I thought hers a most delectable head and not at all one to be forgotten. I watched her perfect movements as she packed her last things away.

'Now where were we going?'

The idea that we were going anywhere was new to me. It was one that terrified me while exciting me beyond measure.

'You did say we were going out to lunch?' she said, obviously puzzled.

'I... er... I've got sandwiches. Out on the Downs perhaps - if you want to, that is.'

And then a feeling gripped me. It was as if a part of me that had never stirred before had taken over my brain.

'Er... or perhaps the little pub. In that village on the Downs. We could have a proper meal. I'll pay.'

Rosie looked up surprised. Then she smiled and linked her arm with mine.

'Lead me on soldier,' she said.

It was the fulfilment of an incredible dream to be sitting in the restaurant portion of a country pub with a beautiful creature like Rosie. My role was one of devoted slave but I hoped that my appearance was one of suitor, even husband. What an absurd thought. How could anyone hold Rosie. Rosie whose generosity was so well known.

Rosie chose a small round table in a corner by the window overlooking the Downs. It was so small that she seemed very near and the small cleft at the top of her blouse appeared to be inches from my face.

She talked of commonplace things in a tuneful voice that was anything but commonplace and as she did so I watched the cleft of the top of her blouse with fascination. Under the table her legs brushed against mine - so little room was there. It was a closeness that terrified me while I relished it.

Outside the sun beat down and, as we left, Rosie suggested that we sit on the grass just watching the mood of the Downs changing in the after rain while a hazy mist from the damp earth greeted the sun.

Whether it was the beer I had consumed (somewhat more than I was used to), or the unusual size of the meal, I fell asleep. And when I woke Rosie's sleeping form was nestled against me. The sun was still shining brightly and my heart rebelled against my mind's consciousness of time.

My mind was working sufficiently to prevent me from looking at my watch; I could justly claim that I had not noticed the time passing.

And I could not move without moving Rosie. I eased my arm which she had pinned to the ground and she stirred. But it was only a small movement and she nestled more closely into my body as if finding in me a haven in which to sleep.

But having moved my arm I was able to support myself on it and look down at Rosie's body. At her beautiful face so close to mine. At that cleavage of which more was showing now that her body was on its side. At her skirt which had ridden up to reveal her long shapely legs. At her feet encased in stiletto high heeled shoes, one of which was hanging half off.

I bent down to ease it back onto her foot and, in doing so, my hand brushed against her leg. I carefully scanned her face but my movement had not disturbed her. I ran my hand up her leg, surprised by the prickly feel of her stockings, and stared at her peaceful face, ashamed that I had defiled her sleep.

While she slept I watched her, watched her breasts move as she breathed deeply, soundly asleep. I wondered if I might kiss her. I knew she would not mind. I bent my face and kissed her chastely on the cheek and then, as if her breasts beckoned me to do so, on the foothills of her breasts at that tantalising spot at which her bosom began to grow.

114

It was this that awakened her. I watched her stirring like a guilty schoolboy.

'I'm sorry I...'

She stared at me sleepily.

'You were asleep,' I said stupidly.

Suddenly she sat up.

'What's the time?' she said.

I looked at my watch. I told her it was four o'clock. I said it quite calmly because it was of no importance to me.

'But we're...' The enormity of her crime settled upon her. 'We must get back.'

But as she rose her lips brushed against mine and she muttered playfully:

'I've loved sleeping with you.'

I never denied the accusations of my fellow members of staff. The delightful thought that I had made love to that adorable creature remained with me until I also believed it to have been true. And when I was summoned to the office of a senior member of staff I had something of the feeling that I had experienced when I was first caned at school. I was terrified of the likelihood of punishment but proud of the guilt that had made me a man.

I can remember snatches of that conversation: 'Disgraceful... know you were led on... have a bright career ahead of you... spoil it all for a few moments... half past four was no time to return to work...'

I let it all wash over me.

But the outcome of the interview was that Rosie was to be moved - a move which I ultimately discovered was due to an earlier liaison with a more senior member of staff who felt the move would be in his own best interests.

But at the time I thought that I was responsible for her removal.

I never saw Rosie again and she remains now as she was then. Her image is unchanged by the passage of years; I never discovered her irritating habits. I never arrived, tired, from work to find she had bought a dress we could not afford. I never discovered her flirting with the next door neighbour. And so, for me, she would never do any of these things. She remains the essential Rosie, and I think of her when I wish to be reassured that God's in his heaven and all's right with the world.

Variation on a Theme by Hardy

The youth who stood outside St Mark's Church was given his first challenge in life when his parents christened him Percival Lancelot Augustus. It was to be the first of many before which he had quailed and retired in defeat. For, although a young man whose character was good (if not strong) and whose appearance was personable, bordering on handsome, he had suffered throughout his eighteen years from a timidity which many believed to be unequalled.

Those holding this opinion were not to be numbered amongst the pious gathering outside St Mark's Church, for that congregation knew well another with a similar affliction. And it was towards this other person that Percival's eyes often turned. Lucy Fielding was the object of his devotion, a devotion which was unavowed and, Percival believed, unreturned.

Some believed that Miss Fielding's shyness was the attraction for Percival but a more persuasive argument for that youth's judgement was her great beauty. They would have made an attractive pair.

As Percival stood outside St Mark's, flakes of snow began to fall and the congregation, which had gathered outside to discuss matters of local import, began to drift towards the church. Percival was the last to enter and, by this time, a thin covering of snow had settled on his hair and the shoulders of his suit.

The girl preceded Percival and took up a position in the second pew from the back. It was an indication of her timidity that, while seeking the obscurity of the back of the church, she essayed to escape the possibility of being requested to take up the offertory. This was a danger which Percival, throwing away caution in his pursuit of beauty, ignored. His position diagonally behind the object of his admiration afforded him an enviable opportunity to study Lucy Fielding at close hand.

The congregation rose and swept vigorously into the opening hymn, while Percival continued his surveillance.

Lucy's body was encased in a thin white cotton dress which was gathered at the neck and tapered to the waist. This caused an admirable tightness around her young bosom, which heaved gently as the words of her song of praise took shape.

Percival watched the dark ridge at the base of the stained glass window as the snow built up upon the ledge outside. He looked down at his hymn book and joined in the second verse:

'Take my hands and let them move
'At the impulse of thy love,
'Take my feet and let them be
'Swift and beautiful for thee.'

His voice tailed away on the word 'beautiful' as the girl picked up her coat and draped it around her shoulders.

'Take my voice and let me sing...'

Percival, feeling that he had been admonished, resumed his song, noticing that the girl's singing was so quiet as to be nearly inaudible. He listened closely; he could just hear her. If only she would sing more loudly. She had a beautiful voice.

It was a sentiment with which not all would have agreed, based as it was on the slender evidence of barely discernible sound and the movement of her lips.

Adorable lips!

'...Take my heart it is Thine own.'

Percival rested his hymn book on the ledge of the pew in front of him. He no longer made any pretence of singing. She glanced to one side; he looked away. She gazed into her hymn book and again he turned his eyes upon her.

'Take my love...' sang the congregation in accord with the youth's feelings.

'Take my self, and I will be
'Ever only, all for Thee.
'Amen.'

'Amen,' sang Percival decisively and reddened as several pairs of eyes turned towards him.

For several minutes his own attention was apparently completely occupied by the words of the hymn he had just completed with such gusto. It may have been that his hymn book was a refuge into which he would, if capable, have climbed to escape attention.

A week after the service, Percival returned to worship. On this occasion the weather was warmer and Lucy Fielding made no recourse to outer garments in order to defeat the winter chill. Her choice of dress may have caused surprise in some of the congregation; indeed whispers about its unsuitability could plainly be heard by Percival, safely ensconced in his back pew.

Percival thought the girl's choice of clothing admirable. For the eyes of a piously bowed head could see clearly the glorious curve of her legs while an intense intercession with his Maker could reveal to Percival a delicate ankle and pretty foot, fashionably shod in high heeled shoes.

Whereas the congregation could have forgiven the brevity of the material coverage of Lucy's legs, it was unable to condone the correspondingly scanty covering of her torso.

No prayer, however fervent, could reveal to Percival the foothills of those beautiful young breasts; this delight was restricted to worshippers in every pew but those occupied by the youth and Lucy Fielding herself.

What met Percival's eyes was an expanse of creamy white skin and with this he made himself content.

How close it was. How easy it would be to hold out a hand to touch...

The sermon droned on, its message disregarded by Percival in his pursuit of happiness.

'The symbol of marriage,' the vicar was saying.

Why the symbol of marriage? Was it an allegory? A metaphorical allusion to the unity between Christ and His church?

Percival was prepared to abandon this conjecture but the association of ideas caused his eyes to rove from the girl's shoulder down her cotton clad arms to the place at which her body re-emerged at the wrist. For a moment he gazed at her long tapering fingers and particularly at the third finger of her left hand on which shone a diamond - set with a cluster of amethysts on an ornate ring.

Percival felt the anger rising within him. He would speak to her. He would not allow her to give herself away so readily. She was too young and only he could love her and cherish her in the way she deserved. Only he would worship her...

The voice from the pulpit echoed around the church with a dirge-like resonance. The girl fingered her ring, obviously unused to wearing it, while members of the congregation shuffled uncomfortably in seats that had caused discomfort to countless generations of worshippers.

Percival felt a tap on his shoulder and a whispered voice said: 'I wonder if you'd mind?'

Percival stared.

'The offertory. I wonder if you'd mind taking it?'

Percival stammered:

'N-n-no.'

'Just up the back pews and collect it in the middle. Usual cut.'

The man grinned. Percival nodded and took the offertory plate.

Mechanically he rose and stood by the pew end. The girl sat three yards from him. He should say something to her. He entered the pew and walked slowly towards her. He stooped, offered the plate and said nothing.

As the girl put in a coin, her arm touched his. For a moment the youth felt paralysed. The girl was looking at him as if waiting. He did not return her look but said:

'Thank you. I... thank you' and stumbled backwards, falling over a prayer cushion and supporting himself to the end of the pew by holding on to the pew in front.

The rest of the offertory passed without incident. But Percival felt that his last chance of happiness had gone.

No one knew where Percival went after the service. There were rumours that he had killed himself for love - these were mainly based on the account of one member of the congregation who had noticed his face as he emerged from the church gate. His expression, according to this witness, suggested a person in suicidal frame of mind.

Lucy Fielding was seventeen; she had emerged from the plumpness of girlhood into the fullness of beauty and possessed a physical maturity unusual for one of her age.

Strangely she had never been seen courting; people were able to provide many reasons for her lack of male company, but probably the only genuine one was her extreme shyness.

This shyness prevented her from declaring her admiration for a young man she saw every week at church. And, indeed, she had been seen, waiting by the bus stop to watch him walking by; her eyes on these occasions, if report is to be believed, moist with tears.

She told only one person about her affection for the youth, and that person, conscience-stricken that he had not told the boy about it, had not revealed the fact until much later when many members of the congregation suddenly remembered events which seemed to have had little significance at the time of their occurrence.

Perhaps the saddest event in this sorry tale occurred when Lucy, frustrated by her shyness, and the youth's apparent lack of interest, began to wear an engagement ring inherited from her mother in token of an affection that would never allow her to give her love elsewhere.

*Although the details of the above story differ greatly from them, the theme is based on a series of notes, prepared by Thomas Hardy. Hardy's story was never written, perhaps because he, after repeated attempts, could not decide the form in which to write it. The irony of the wearing of the ring, central to the story, is an invention of Hardy's.

Sonia of The Tower

For a time Mr Lawrence watched the boats passing on the river. They appeared suddenly out of the mist and as dramatically were gone. He passed a hand across his forehead wiping the sweat that had gathered and, picking up his brief case, walked back along the tree lined path to the newspaper shop.

The shop door bell rang and a woman of about thirty looked up. He placed his briefcase on the counter and said with the force of habit:

'*Financial Times* please.'

'Has to be got special,' said the woman.

'Oh I see.'

'Goin' to the station?'

'Yes. Yes I am.'

'Get 'em at the station. You ain't a reg'lar are yer?'

'No I am not. Actually I am a...'

'No, I thought not. We only order for reg'lars, see.'

'Oh yes. Oh I see.'

Mr Lawrence clicked his brief case, shut and pulled it off the counter.

'Ain't seen yer 'ere. I gets ter know faces,' the assistant said.

'I suppose you would, yes. I did live here.'

'Oh I see - before I come back 'ere. More 'n five years?'

'Oh good heavens yes,' smiled Mr Lawrence. 'It would be twenty. More than twenty.' Then he realised that he did not know exactly how long it had been.

'Well I reckon I wouldn't know yer. Here as a boy was yer?' Mr Lawrence took the compliment with a smile.

'Rather more than that I'm afraid.' He tugged at the brim of his bowler and walked to the door.

'Name ain't Lawrence is it?' the woman shouted after him. He looked round slowly, then said:

'No, I'm afraid not. No, it's not Lawrence.'

He walked to the bus stop wondering how the assistant had known his name. It was just a guess of course. A lucky guess.

The bus journey took him out of the old forest and through the council housing estate to the station.

He had a dislike of revealing his identity. But the assistant's words pursued him. He had lived there, he pondered, and she had heard his name. That was all. She probably wondered whether he was the man who... No, that was not the answer; your name does not live on for twenty - thirty? - yes, more like thirty years. Why the woman was probably not even born when he had journeyed as a twenty five year old to take up his position in the Civil Service and left the area in favour of a one-roomed apartment in Ealing.

The day passed in much the same way as the day before. And the day before that. Except that today the prospect of the evening held more excitement for him for he felt he must return. His desk reminded him of the years he had wasted; the village... the village made him think of what might have been. So tonight he would not catch the Central Line train to Ealing but walk to nearby Victoria Station.

When he arrived at the village he made his way purposefully from the bus stop, skirted the main cluster of houses and walked through the woods to a building in the clearing. It had once been the workshop of an astronomer but Mr Lawrence's own past was closely connected with it and he approached with a feeling akin to reverence.

The tower had its history but it was one in which he had hitherto shown little interest: to him the important part of the structure's existence had occurred during his lifetime.

He approached the door with apprehension, but the thrill of returning to the tower and the proximity of a building that represented so important a part of his life (he felt this in retrospect) excited him. He walked round to a lower window and pushed his fingers under the metal adjoining the cill, sliding his hand inside. At first he thought that it had gone. He had no right to expect it to be there after all these years... but the key was there. With his index finger he looped it from its hook and, with a quick glance over his shoulder, walked back to the door and inserted the key in the lock.

The lock had obviously not seen the key for many years. Mr

Lawrence turned it impatiently but was eventually rewarded by the sound of a click as the bolt flew across. He opened the door and stared into the tower's gloomy interior. When his eyes had adjusted to the darkness he carefully mounted the stairs and pushed open the door of an upper storey room.

It was exactly as he remembered it, lit only by a windowed aperture in the roof from which the ancient astronomer had viewed the heavens. The room was bare but for the metal fixture with two side arms which had held the telescope of the tower's earlier occupant and a rude bench on which he had presumably sat to assimilate the results of his observations.

Mr Lawrence had been sitting for some time before he noticed the locket. And even then he was tempted to disregard it - until the realisation struck him that it might be hers. No one surely had entered the tower since his last visit. His heart thumped against his chest as he picked it up and opened it.

The picture at which he stared was that of a young woman of no more than eighteen. His head spun and his hands reached out for the support which, in the event, failed him. He fell forward and his knees buckled under him. In his head beat an almost tribal tattoo and, slowly, the ground seemed to swallow him.

The voices appeared to come from nowhere. From behind closed eyes his subconscious heard them. Young voices. A girl.

'You will not go to London?'

He grasped the air in front of him. There was nothing.

'I must go, Sonia,' he heard his own voice saying. 'There I have a future. Here I have nothing.'

Suddenly two figures appeared.

The girl smiled sadly resting her hand upon those of a young man in a neat suit.

'Then you must,' she said. 'And I will be brave but...'

'But?'

Her fingers were nervously unbuttoning the buttons of her blouse.

'Sonia! Sonia!'

'If you are never to come home.'

'I didn't say that.'

'But you know it to be true. You will never come back.'

Mr Lawrence watched her as the last article of her clothing dropped to the floor - as he had watched her long ago when they had made love for the first and only time. It had been her parting gift. But what had those moments of ecstasy meant to him - the villager to whom the lights of London had called? The man who had made himself an empire in a filing registry. He felt bile rising to his mouth and the pain in his head returned.

'Sonia?' he said quietly knowing there would be no reply.

'Sonia,' he said again shaking his head and resisting the tears that were forming in his eyes. He looked around the room. It was empty and the tower was a tower of ghosts.

He looked down at the picture in the locket and turned it over in his hand. He had not noticed the inscription on the back.

'I knew you would return,' he read, and put it quickly aside. So she had not believed what she had said. That gargantuan goodbye had not been a finale but a promise. She had thought he would return to her. Well, in a manner of speaking he had. But perhaps this had been the type of return she had envisaged?

A noise below caught his attention. For one moment he thought that Sonia had returned. But of course that could not be. It was news of her death that had brought him here. Nothing else would have done so.

He heard the door open and steps on the stairs. An absurd panic seized him and he grabbed the telescope stand for support.

'Mr Lawrence,' shouted a voice.

He knew her then. It was the woman from the newspaper shop and hers was an intrusion he resented.

'I thought I said that I was not Mr...'

'Not Mr Lawrence? Yes, but I know diff'rent. Who else would come to the tower? Only me mum and... and Mr Lawrence. She told me - about the courtin' and that. It must have been bad for 'er. You having to leave.'

'Your mother?'

The woman ignored him.

'I was born here but we moved to a place in Clapham. She wanted to come back and I didn't mind.'

'But... she had a child. She met someone after me and...'

'She met no one.'

'It would have been perfectly reasonable; I will not feel offended if you tell me she met another man and she had a... a... child... well she had you.'

'She met no one,' the woman repeated.

Mr Lawrence sat on the bench.

'I never thought...'

'No, me mum thought that perhaps you never thought.'

Mr Lawrence rose with a sigh.

'And now you have come to reproach me?'

The woman looked genuinely surprised.

'Me mum said if ever you was to come back I was to invite you to come to the shop. You know she died?'

'Yes, yes, I know that.'

'And you'll come to the shop?'

Mr Lawrence's funeral was quite an event in the village. His success as a shopkeeper - the expansion of his empire - completely outshone his career in the city - made him a celebrity. But if he was respected he was little loved. He was not one to attract affection and would not have known what to do with it had he done so.

And his visits to the tower made him a curiosity. Few would have guessed that he had enough romance in him to remember a lost love, and few saw any irony in the demolition of the building on the day his body made its last journey from the village.

The Bully

I could hear the ringing sound of the children playing at the playground fountain. Most of them had gone straight into school; it was such a cold morning. I had my catapult-shaped twig and could use my time well until the school bell went.

I twiddled the twig in a spider's web on the hedge. When it emerged I had a patterned tracery in the cleft of my twig, the frost having painted a diamond-like glitter on its surface which twinkled in the weak early morning sun.

I planted my twig in the ground under the hedge where I should be able to find it the next morning. It was a good twig and I did not wish to lose it. If I took it into school, it might be taken; boys wanted twigs like that.

I took up a bigger stick and ran it along the railings making a satisfying chinking noise. Then I discarded the stick and ran the tips of my fingers along; it made little sound but produced a strange sensation in the finger tips.

The school bell sounded.

I rushed in through the school gates and vaulted over the wooden fence which ran alongside the driveway. I joined my queue and waited to file into school. I could see him in another queue. I tried to avoid his eyes but he had spotted me. His eyes told me that he realised I had delayed until the last moment to join the queue. He knew why. The teacher on duty waited until more genuine late comers had filed into place; then we walked into school.

As I passed by The Boy a stone hit the side of my face; I was half expecting it but the stone hurt and I had difficulty in holding back the tears.

Playtimes were spent in constant fear of The Bully. Looking back, I must have played a small part in his life; I was merely his current victim. The fact that I kept out of his way, spent most of my playtimes in the toilet, probably pleased him and he made no great effort to seek me out. But, after football that day, we were changing when his class came out.

I tried to avoid him. If I could finish dressing before he passed I could lose myself in the crowd and leave without his seeing me. But luck was not on my side and he spotted me.

I continued to dress as if nothing was wrong. But I was aware of him approaching. He picked up my football boots and threw them over the fence. I said nothing and went to retrieve them.

When I returned he pushed me. By this time a crowd had gathered. Boys were pushing for a better view.

It was then I realised that, in my fear, I had put my pullover on back to front. This simple fact saved me from accusations of cowardice later since my pulling off of the pullover was interpreted as a preparation for the fight. It also, I was later to discover, raised my stock in the eyes of my tormentor.

But it did not move him to pity. A situation had developed where he and I faced each other inside a ring of eager onlookers. I took the pullover and turned it right way round. This part of the story was never told if it was noticed. My intention was still to put the pullover on, replace my jacket, and make for home.

But his fist connected with the side of my face. I reeled against the fence. As if in a daze I buttoned the cuff of my shirt.

'Let him get ready,' someone said. 'Give him a chance.'

In a moment he was on me. He swung wildly but his fist connected with the wooden fence behind me. I had taken no evasive action. It was simply a wild punch.

I still just wanted to go home and, for the second time that day, was very close to tears; I pushed him off. He stumbled and fell back. I knew if I kicked or hit him, it would anger him sufficiently for him to continue the fight. I smiled - an expression which scarcely reflected my feelings, replaced my pullover and jacket and walked through the ring of spectators. My tormentor picked himself up and made to follow me.

'Come on Bal. Leave him. We've got to get ready for the game.'

'Bal' left me. I walked home unseeing and unhearing.

The incident, years later, became a family story. It was presented as a victory for the gallant David against the bully Goliath. A passing parent had recounted what she saw of the skirmish (I could hardly claim a fight since I had not aimed one punch) and what she had seen had developed into a tale of uncaring heroism. The pullover incident had been carefully noted, showing coolness under pressure, and my leaving had suggested that the incident had been little to me - a small part of the rich life of a schoolboy.

The next morning I had retrieved my twig and was creating jewelled patterns with it in the spiders' webs. The school bell rang and, with even greater reluctance than usual, I ran into the playground.

I spotted him in the other queue as I formed up. As usual I ignored him although I was very much aware of his presence. As I filed into school I braced myself for a missile. But none came.

I was as cautious as usual at playtime but, when the time arrived to return to the building, I emerged from the toilets at precisely the time that he was entering them. For a moment we stopped, staring at each other. Then he inclined his head slightly, said 'Hi,' and continued on his way.

Echoes of Sandy Patch

Laura was apparently happily married. Certainly none of her neighbours had seen her fighting with her husband; I had no evidence that she ever did. It was just a feeling, and a knowledge of the girl as she was when, as an eighteen year old, she had been my constant companion. I could not see *that* Laura, submitting easily to the tyrannies of a husband who... but there again I was conjecturing: Laura told me nothing. All that she did was to take her small son shopping every Friday evening and allow me to take him for the evening while she, as was wholly proper, showed none of the old signs of affection nor any inclination to talk over old times.

Of course my pride was hurt, but my consolation was in the boy, to whom I showed the play places of my own childhood: the boy who looked so much as I had looked - the boy who was my son.

Paul showed great interest in Sandy Patch, a dying but still fascinating corner of the park with which progress had not yet caught up, and there we sailed his yacht and swung in the lower branches of the trees. On one occasion I misdirected his yacht - a brash blue affair which Laura's husband had bought him - and watched helpless as it smashed itself against the rocks of the waterfall and tumbled with the water into the pools below. I had watched his face expecting tears to well up but none came. He simply looked up at me expectantly and I took his hand and we hurried to the shops. There I bought him a boat - less showy but firmly built and red - and we took it back to the stream and watched its maiden voyage through the calm water between patches of waving shadows and glittering, sun-made ripples.

The new boat - Paul christened it 'The Adventurer' - was never misdirected. But on several occasions Paul rushed to steer it well clear of the intake of water which formed at the top of the falls, and into the calm waters of the stream by our own bank.

When first Paul took the boat home I wondered whether it

would occasion any remark, but when Laura met me again the following Friday, none was passed, nor was there any more conversation made than Laura felt was absolutely necessary.

Later I asked her about it but she was non-committal. Her husband had not noticed the new boat as any different from the one he had bought; Laura had noticed but not cared. What I bought my son was my business, she had said, and, in that way, she was very fair. She considered that I had rights in the matter which was strange since Paul had been born since her marriage. Perhaps it was all an effort to salve her own conscience: I was unable to tell.

However her conscience never extended as far as her husband and this seemed so unlike Laura that I simply knew that he must ill-treat her.

As Paul grew older his interests tended the way mine had done. Instead of tinkering with mechanical things, like Laura's husband, he set out on long treks to find prehistoric hill-forts, ancient castles and the lonely stones of Neolithic burials. Of all his adventures he would tell me on our Friday meetings and I, in turn, would try to build a story around his tombs and fortresses, people them with giants and mighty warriors and erect on the bare earth the flags of a conqueror and on their crumbling walls a story of the past.

But when Paul was ten his mother ruled that I should not see him again. It had been alright when she had been able to visit her mother in London but now that her mother had died her excuse had gone, and she felt no compunction to visit the capital.

It was a sad time for I realised that, much as I enjoyed Paul's company, the fact that he was my one remaining link with Laura was the most important consideration in our relationship.

At first I accepted the situation and let Paul explore his Dorset countryside alone, but then, without the consolation of his friendship, my mind turned more and more towards his mother, until one rainy November day found me on a train bound for Dorset.

I had little trouble finding her and, when I did, it was sufficient. For a time I watched her on her walks and, once or twice, I followed her.

I stayed in Dorchester until December and then I let Laura know that I was there. She showed no reaction, either of surprise, or pleasure, but she did agree to my meeting Paul again.

It was then that I decided to kill Laura's husband. I regarded him as an animal and I made my plans with the same cold detachment with which someone else would prepare to swat a fly. The plan was not a complicated one; I went to none of the great lengths to avoid detection that would seem necessary for a modern criminal; I merely waited for him to take his customary walk to Poundbury and hit him with an iron bar. The ghosts of Poundbury protected me; I felt their eyes on me as I walked away from his body.

I did not leave Dorchester and the investigations into Laura's husband's death did not touch me. Nor did I meet Laura or Paul for some time after but, when I did, people considered it natural that an attractive widow should have found a lover.

But Laura did not treat me as a lover. Even when we married - an event which Laura accepted with the air of one acknowledging the inevitable - she showed none of her old happiness and Paul alone cheered me through the dark years of our marriage. By the time Paul was sixteen, Laura had taken on the appearance of a machine. If she had human feelings, she successfully hid them. I tried to be kind but my kindness was met with the same aloofness as my anger; I tried to change her but she would not be changed. I became embittered, realising that this was the relationship for which I had killed a man. I never regretted killing him because, rightly or wrongly, I blamed him for the creation of this new Laura. I thought of the gay laughter of her teenage self and saw that most of her laughter had become her son. Paul was the embodiment of our relationship as well as its outcome and yet he seemed oblivious of the fact that his father had been murdered and his mother dehumanised.

I watched Paul and his efficient handling of girls several years older than himself. I watched him embark on the spring of his years with a feeling which was akin to envy. Then I remembered how he had learnt it all from me and felt better.

My last days in Dorset were spent in Paul's company. I drank with him and shared his women. And I talked with him about his mother for he, too, had wondered what had happened to her. Although it did not seem to trouble him, I was not prepared for the remark he made one evening. He raised his pint glass and, with a wink, said:

'Shall we kill *her* then, Dad?'

Life, Death and After Life of Herbert Cleake

The day was appropriately fine when Herbert and Mary Cleake moved into the home that they had planned since their first meeting in an air raid shelter in Balham some years before.

Their union was universally believed to be ideal. By friends (who pointed out their shared interests) and by others who, with perhaps more accuracy, argued that they were both 'a bit odd'.

Herbert Cleake's affection for his wife at this time was undeniable although the process of his disillusionment - which was to result in his developing a marked coldness in the face of his wife's undying devotion - was quickly to make itself apparent.

He had designated a section of their garden as his own and spent much of his leisure time - of which his life largely consisted - in writing philosophy based on a scanty knowledge of the concepts of Plato. He was known, indeed, to have read *The Republic* - at least a tattered Everyman edition of it was frequently to be found in the house, lying as if recently put aside.

Mary Cleake subsequently remembered wistfully the early days of their marriage when her husband would invite her to his 'summer house' after his day's labour with the pen and they would walk in the fields nearby and watch the seasonal colours of the trees changing from green to brown.

For reasons which must be the concern only of the couple themselves, the relationship was never consummated, although Mary's devotion permitted no resulting rancour to enter her mind. And she traced her husband's chequered career with an interest which its mediocrity scarcely warranted.

Cleake had been employed in many capacities but preferred to think of himself as an ex-civil servant because of a few weeks undistinguished service to the Home Office. His most difficult job had been to convince publishers that he was a philosopher. The polite response was that philosophy was no longer a marketable commodity: those less polite had been heard to argue that philosophy was philosophy whereas Herbert Cleake's philosophy was something else again.

His reason for deciding that the Home Office was not for him - a conclusion to which he had come at about the same time as his employer - was that he was reluctant to work as part of a system. He felt this suppressed his individuality and stifled his genius. But with the belief inherent in all great men he relied on Posterity to claim him from the morass of writers which this age has proclaimed failures.

His self-assurance did not, however, pay the bills: this was a task that Herbert Cleake felt more suited to his wife. Cleake returned to the 'summer house' and his writings accrued at an alarming rate.

As with other great men Herbert Cleake developed a sense of despondency. He saw no reason why he should share his thoughts with lesser mortals, especially as the majority lacked the capacity to appreciate them.

And a strange, and some felt uncharacteristic, desire came upon him to climb in the Rockies. The fervent wish became an obsession. His wife accepted it as she accepted all else her husband did and, when it came, she accepted his decision to pack his bags and cross the Atlantic with all the fortitude of a saint.

Continued fortitude was required when the news came, as it soon did, of his death in a climbing accident. Had people heard of this tragedy they might have argued that it was to be expected that Cleake's mountaineering would be as unconventional as his philosophy - and the outcome, as a result, predictable.

But they did not. Mary Cleake refused to accept the death of one she believed imperishable and continued to write to him and to send money which continued to be gratefully received - a fact which confirmed Mary in the belief that her husband was yet living.

And when she was notified that Herbert Cleake's body would be flown home, she prepared to meet not a body but her dear living husband. At the funeral parlour which she visited daily, she was permitted to view his body. She had however to accept that the face she saw was hideously transformed. A great change had come over Herbert Cleake.

The change was soon accepted and, when the required customary interment was completed, she lingered long after the last mourner

– there were very few – had left, and prepared to undertake a vigil at his grave.

Mary Cleake started to sleep in the 'summer house' - however cold or wet the night - in the knowledge that, since this was his favoured place, she was near her husband. Even closer was she when she visited his grave in the local cemetery, and so it happened that, three days after her husband's melancholy interment, she began to feel hands gripping her bare, cold arms. The hands moved to her back and ran lightly down her body. Mary was unafraid. She had expected something like this.

Each day her husband - for surely it was he - became more bold. Although she could not see him she was aware of his light pressure on her wrist. It was how he had always held her before kissing her in the days before his ardour had died. She felt cold lips upon hers and wondered at the increase in his passion. She was inclined to sympathy. He probably had little else to do.

Although Mary Cleake continued to work in a High Street milliners, her time after her return home was monopolised by the attention of a man who required no food nor drink and who treated her with a kindness hitherto unknown. It was hardly surprising that her colleagues and neighbours began to notice a change in her. Once again – after a period of many years - she was happy.

It was therefore with great surprise that neighbours learned of the discovery of her body in the cemetery; it should have come as no surprise that it was found on the grave of her late spouse.

And a premature verdict of suicide while of unsound mind was reached. Certainly no one would have believed that she had died in the happy and unlikely belief that her husband had again truly loved her and that, together in a state of complete union, they had ascended the celestial ladder to the stars.

Just Outside Victoria Station

We looked at the snow outside. Flakes melted on the glass of the window; others formed a slight covering on the ledge.

The old lady looked at us and said:

'How nice it is that you have come to see me. So few do.'

Linda reached for the old lady's hand and held it in her own.

'I wanted to show him to you,' she said.

'And so right to do so my dear. These men are so necessary. I so nearly had one myself.'

She looked at me and her eyes sparkled.

'I am too old to claim any knowledge of a man by sight; too many people think they can do that. But he will do you. He will make a good husband.'

Linda looked at the wrinkled hand she held in her lap.

'You said you nearly...'

'Had a man myself.' Her laugh was more of a chuckle, and the mischievous schoolgirl was dominant in her when she chuckled. 'If you would like to hear about him...?'

'Not if it would cause you...'

'Oh, don't say pain my dear. Everyone thinks old people suffer the pain of reminiscences. But why do so many people indulge themselves in nostalgia? Because it is a pleasurable pain, my dear, and one we would not miss for the world. No, I am only worried that you will be bored - I am told young people are so easily bored today. And no wonder. With so much not to do you have time for monotony and boredom.'

She withdrew her hand from Linda's hold and poured tea into cups of Victorian china. As she took her own she leant forward in her seat, her cup of tea poised like a pointer with which a commander would outline battle tactics.

'I was born in a little village in Kent. I do not remember its name and I always make a point of forgetting the date.' She took a sip

136

of tea.

'Until I was eighteen I had never really looked at a boy although I had thought enough about them, and, at that age, one of the villagers summoned enough courage to ask my parents (it was done like that then) if he could walk out with me.

'He was rather a spotty youth and I did not share the (well hidden) eagerness which, my parents assured me, had urged him to his proposal. But we did walk together in the frosted fields although I don't think he noticed them in wondering what he should say or, heaven preserve us, what he should do!

'I remember how the sun made pearls of the frost and how the damp air coated our eye lids with sparkling drops which stung the eyes. My companion changed: he became a partner in an adventure and I looked upon him with different eyes.

'But this feeling waned. As he struggled to make conversation I wished myself alone, and soon he lost his nerve altogether and bad me good day saying he had seen a friend.

'The departure (even by modern standards) was rude and unfeeling. But I saw him for what he was: an immature youth whose parents had decided that the least flighty girl in the village would be the most suitable for their son, and forgave him on those grounds. But I thanked him in my heart for the hitherto unexpected freedom with which he had left me.

'And as I walked along the meadow lanes, schemes began to fill my mind and I,' she chuckled again, 'began to formulate a plan whereby I could enjoy this freedom more often. If you ask, my dear, what a girl was doing at the age of eighteen accepting the limitations placed by her parents and not even daring to walk the lanes without company of their choosing, I can only remind you that times were very different then.'

The old lady looked from me to Linda's short skirt and smiled when the latter attempted to pull down the hem to a more decorous level.

'Anyway, I chased after the youth whose name, I remember, was John, and arrested his attention in a most unladylike fashion. I suggested that he should inform his parents that our meeting had been successful and that we had decided upon further walks. This suited our plans equally well while limiting our "walks" to the neighbourhood where my parents would not insist on a chaperone. Do not smile my dear.

'Our actual meetings from here on were brief. We would see each other only for a few moments before going our separate ways and, after a month, John did not appear at all. This destroyed the truth of my story but did not diminish my enjoyment of walking.

'I heard later that John had lost his pimples and his shyness and had used his freedom to rather better effect than I. Or is that possible? Could anyone have been more full of bliss than I as I walked the lanes (whatever the weather) my hand firmly grasped by the man of my dreams - a man who had grown out of that pimply and far off John and who had inherited his name.

'Presumably John returned to his parents after his "walks" and his stories must have been plausible enough to satisfy them. As for me, I did not need to invent, for I believed my role and painted my companion in glowing colours - my parents thought this a sign of love and a pointer to our marriage.

'But no proposal came and they worried. They asked me if John was well and I answered that he was, and described him - a description so unlike its original that even my parents showed signs of surprise.

'Then came the terrible news. John had been killed. The news of his death came with a friend of his who had travelled down from London. Gossip soon spread. He had been killed in a brawl in a disreputable house - you know my dear - and then in a street fight. But when the newspapers carried the story, his death assumed more normal proportions. He had been killed when his train had been de-railed just outside Victoria Station.

'Surprisingly I received much sympathy. It was supposed that he had broken our tryst and my parents never doubted that I had been seeing him for what had been nearly a year.

'But despite the sympathy which I did not deserve I was not to be comforted. Although the youth with whom I had walked on that frosty morning meant nothing to me, the companion of my walks had grown out of him and bore his name. When, on a bitterly cold day, I was taken to see his grave, I stood impassively before the snow-shrouded tomb. Only later did the tears come, for what was buried in that grave was my freedom and, more importantly, the only man I had ever loved.'

The old lady pulled back the curtain so that she could see into the garden. She watched the snow drifting lazily down onto the blanket of whiteness which covered the ground.

Then she noticed that her tea had grown cold and placed it back on the tray.

'It is the first time I have told the true story, my dear,' she said and then looked at me, 'and how lucky you are, my love, to have found a real one.'

Jenny in Black

Carder looked up at the sun.

'It wasn't always like this,' he said.

Mr Wapshott lowered his paper by inches and replied:

'Not always like this son?'

'Not always lonely. You know.'

'You're lonely?'

'Certainly.'

'With a lovely wife and...'

'Kids crawling round the house, tearing my papers, ruining my books.'

'And when was it better, then, boy?'

'When I was sixteen. When love was...'

'Infatuation.'

'Nonsense. There is no love like adolescent love.'

Mr Wapshott put the paper down by his side and looked at Carder with renewed interest.

'And your adolescent loves, boy. They were...'

'Superb, quite superb. I remember one...'

Carder looked up but Mr Wapshott had not returned to his paper. He was actually listening. Carder gulped at the thought of the interest thus implied.

'You see, Jenny.'

'Nice name Jenny.'

'But you should have seen her. She had dark hair and...'

Carder stopped. He could remember Jenny clearly but he could not describe her. He searched for words. 'She beggars description.'

'I know,' said Mr Wapshott, 'There are some girls like that.'

'There can't be many. Not like Jenny.'

'No. Not many. I've never found one.'

Carder noticed that the 'son' and the 'boy' had been dropped.

The condescending attitude had gone. He rested his head back on his hands and watched the sun flickering through the upper branches of the trees on its path over their heads.

'It was a day like this.'

'When you met?'

'No. No. I met her in a youth club. The sunny day was when we...'

Mr Wapshott nodded: 'I understand.'

Carder was certain he did not understand. His sixteen year old self had viewed the girl's body with the eyes of a worshipper. Only now could he consider violation of that sacred flesh with anything but horror. Now he would give anything to... but he was sixteen then, and Mr Wapshott was muttering something about wild oats.

'Only to be expected,' said Mr Wapshott more loudly. 'A boy of that age and a girl, well, like that.'

The sun had at last emerged from the tree tops. Carder lifted his hand to shield his eyes from its glare.

'I used to call her Jenny in Black,' he said. 'She used to wear a black trouser suit. When she wore a skirt instead, it was...well she had beautiful legs and...'

'Yes,' said Mr Wapshott. 'I can imagine. And what happened to the girl?'

'I took her to Wales.'

'What did you want to that for?'

'I don't know. But it was a long way away. Nobody would hear and... well, people do go to Wales. No one would think it odd.'

'No, I suppose not. And this sunny day?'

'Well, I'll let you into a secret.'

Mr Wapshott leant forward to hear the confidence although the park was deserted.

'It was here,' Carder said simply.

'This very...!' Mr Wapshott whistled. 'An anniversary?'

'Ten years to the day. This very spot. Yes.'

'But wasn't it, I mean... public.'

'Where I proposed to her.'

'Oh, I see. Mm. Proposed?' he said, as if assimilating facts by degrees. Carder nodded.

Mr Wapshott stared at his forgotten paper.

'She accepted of course. And she is now your...'

'Oh, no,' said Carder.

'She didn't accept?' said Mr Wapshott, his mouth dropping open in surprise.

'She accepted but...'

'Oh dear, another girl came along who...'

Carder nodded. 'And she was...?' He nodded again.

'So you had to...and now she is...?'

'My wife, yes. She became my wife.'

Mr Wapshott picked up his paper and stuffed it into his brief case.

'But you were saying earlier about your wife. She's beautiful of course?'

'Quite beautiful but...'

'Yes, yes, I understand. However beautiful, she will never be...'

Carder was on the brink of tears. Mr Wapshott clicked his brief case shut and rose to his feet.

'Got to go old chap, I'm afraid,' he said. 'Enjoyed our chat. Enjoyed it but - very sorry you know. What a pearl she must have been. And to lose her like that.'

Mr Wapshott seemed unable to find more words. Carder stared at the grass and then at the moving patterns of the trees' shadows; Mr Wapshott was not sure whether he was crying. He moved away quietly, round the fountain and the Gentlemen's toilet. But as he walked out into the main road, he looked back. Carder was still there, his head bent low. Soon he would heave a sigh and shake off his sorrow. Then, as Mr Wapshott well knew, he would return to his dingy bachelor flat in the High Street and read again his favourite volume of love poems.

Baker's Number One Moment

Thank God it was warm in the carriage! Outside the snow was beginning to settle and large flakes glistened like crystals on the window. Baker eased himself down in his seat and drew a magazine from his brief case. He tried to read the words as they jogged before him - but the knees of the girl next to him were the only things in focus. He pulled his eyes back to the page and concentrated - but the knees were more interesting.

Baker looked out of the window and watched the settling snow. With his sleeve he cleaned the misted pane and settled further into his seat.

But the train entered a tunnel and he found himself looking at the reflection of the girl beside him. She was staring at an evening newspaper without reading. Baker looked away; he felt that she must have felt his eyes upon her. He looked again but she showed no sign of having noticed him. What, he wondered, were his chances with a girl like that? Nil. Absolutely nil, he thought as the train emerged from the tunnel and its heightened drumming rhythm softened to a murmured staccato.

Baker's eyes roved. The heavy looking man opposite would have no trouble with her. Nor would the flash executive staring eagerly through his pebble glasses at a copy of the *Financial Times*. But Baker? Not Baker!

Not the boy with the shock of untidy hair who had grown from the gawkiness of adolescence to a totally new form of adult awkwardness for which he had become a by-word.

He had always stooped. People considered this the reason for the precarious angle at which his glasses had always tilted. In fact when, one morning, he appeared at the office spectacle-less and tearful it was assumed that they had fallen off and that, typically, Baker had not noticed. But the contact lenses which had been to Baker a symbol of a new determination had had only a temporary effect on his confidence, for he soon discovered that, with or without spectacles, no girl was interested in him. Some were rude, others were kind but the result was the same: Baker faced the future peering, through long habit, into the quite impossible prospect of romance.

As dusk fell the snow showed with almost fluorescent brilliance. It had taken so little time for the watery layer to become a blanket and, in that time, Baker had reflected on his lost opportunities.

The girl was still staring disinterestedly at her newspaper. And Baker watched her as she flicked over the page and glanced at its contents.

'Hello love!'

Baker swung round. It was the heavy looking man who had spoken. Curse him. How dare he treat this object of Baker's adoration with such arrogance?

The girl smiled but did not look up.

'I said hello,' the heavy man repeated. 'Don't you want to talk to me?' This time the girl looked up, smiled, and said:

'Reading.'

'Reading what? Is it that interesting?'

'It doesn't have to be does it?' the girl replied.

The heavy man rose and took the seat on the other side of the girl from Baker.

'I just thought, if you were interested...'

'No thanks,' said the girl.

'But, really, I know a place...'

'I dare say you do. Really, I'm reading.'

Then Baker noticed the man's hand. He was going to touch her. Baker leant forward to watch as the heavy man's hand reached for the girl's waist.

Suddenly Baker leapt up. In a voice strangely unlike his own he heard himself say:

'You heard what she said. You heard it. I heard it. Leave her alone. Leave her alone.'

The man's hand returned to his pocket and his face swung towards Baker. But the astonishment was momentary.

Baker sat down. He felt hot. He wondered what the man would

do. He waited for a blow, expecting it, but none came. The man did not even speak; he laughed, but Baker did not see that.

Neither did Baker see the man rise, nor hear his merriment as he walked down the corridor. The girl noticed, but Baker sat back timidly in his seat, hearing and seeing nothing.

Then she turned towards him and Baker realised for the first time that they were alone. He stared at her, not knowing what to do. And then, to Baker's astonishment, she pitched forward onto him, apparently in a faint.

Baker took her weight. The closeness of her body excited him. He could see her breasts moving as she breathed. He could see their outline on her blouse and the cleft between them which became more evident as her body fell forward and the neck of her blouse loosened.

What had made him say what he did? And what would he do now? Baker considered - and concluded, with typically Baker logic, that he had best do nothing.

But the girl's breasts were a challenge to him. Baker noticed that she was not wearing a bra and that her beautiful breasts were...

The train slowed and moved into the station... Baker waited. The train received more passengers but no one entered Baker's compartment. He thought with pride that they had chosen to leave lovers to their own devices.

This beautiful girl, this goddess, was his. He felt the movement of her legs and looked at her face. She was coming round. He gently removed his arm from her shoulder. Her eyes opened.

'I... I'm awfully sorry,' she said.

'No, no - quite alright.'

'Silly of me to...'

'No, no, please, it's quite alright...'

Baker dried up.

'And thank you,' she said.

'Thank you? I...'

'For being so brave.'

'O.K. That's alright... er... thank you, I mean...'

Baker gave up and stared out of the window at the bleak winter landscape.

'It's still snowing,' the girl said.

Baker nodded.

'And lying.'

Baker nodded again.

The train slowed again and a familiar name board appeared at the window. Baker lifted her small case down from the rack and carried it to the ticket barrier. Then he stood and watched her offer her ticket and turn out of the station. He did not feel the snow which encased him in a white jacket.

But, by the morning, his spirits had returned

His smile hid his inner knowledge that this goddess had been his, that he could see her as she was for those five glorious minutes. No one could guess how intimately he had held her.

Baker prepared to board the train. The snow was gone but the memory was vivid. Again he smiled.

And she smiled too - to herself.

All the Beautiful Ladies

Having leapt from the wall he waited, crouched low. Before him the house was barely visible through the mist; beside him was a Grecian temple with which an eccentric eighteenth century owner of the house had fulfilled his desire for conformity.

With a nervous look about him, he walked round the wall of the temple, under its Ionic pillars and into its cold interior. The pale sun was increasing in strength; he had been there for some time. The misty sunlight lit his features. He was young - about nineteen or twenty - too old to be a boy but not yet a man.

He seated himself on the stone bench seat. She will not be long, he promised himself; she is always late.

Then he heard the rustle of a dress. He saw her appear from the direction of the house. She had skirted the fore-lawn, preferring to keep to the trees. She spoke:

'I am late.'

'It doesn't matter. You are here.'

Suddenly and surprisingly she laughed:

'Of course it does not. You will come despite. You will always come.'

'You know I will.'

Again the girl laughed.

'To be the object of such passion,' she mocked.

Then her face took on a more serious expression. He could not tell whether she was again mocking him.

'You are not the first,' she said.

'It doesn't matter. It doesn't matter...'

'Oh! Goodness me,' said the girl, clapping her hands, 'you misunderstand me. I do not mean you are not my first lover. Of course you are not. You are not even my lover. Are you dear? I doubt whether you are capable. No, no, I meant that you are not the first to climb over the wall at this spot. Neither are you the first to meet a lady of the house in - ah - clandestine circumstances.'

'I do not care about your other lovers.'

'Oh, not mine. Before you I have been quite open; I have not needed to be otherwise never having toyed with a little boy before. No the lady was my mother.'

'Oh yes, I know about it.'

'There was a murderer you know.'

'Yes he tried but did not succeed by the lake.'

Everyone in the area knew the story. The family had, for a time, tried to hush it up, but it was too delightful and macabre a story to escape local gossip.

She took his chin in her hand.

'Do you wish me to tell you about it?'

'I know. Your mother was courting a man from the village.'

'Courting!' she snorted, 'Courting, my dear Paul. No, she was playing with him, just as I am playing with you. He was about your age, Paul; my mother was about my age. She teased him dreadfully you know. She treated him so badly until...!'

'Until there came a time when he could stand it no more,' he finished... 'until he killed her because he loved her too much to be hurt by her any longer.'

'Is that what they say Paul dear? Could it just have been that he was of peasant stock and a very low creature and that he reverted to the behaviour of an animal?'

'I don't know,' Paul said.

The woman seated herself beside Paul.

'Would you kill me if I drove you too far, Paul?' she asked.

He looked away.

'I think you would,' she said, 'I think you would kill me. You might even enjoy it.'

He did not turn to face her. She spoke again:

'He tried again, you know. He tried again to kill her. He succeeded the second time.'

'I know he succeeded.'

Suddenly the young woman jumped up and clapped her hands:

'I must show you where it all happened. It is all so interesting.'

148

She led him through the trees.

'My mother put the lock on the temple door, you know. That was very thoughtful of her. She did it so that they could be left alone - her and that animal. Poor mother.'

She took Paul's hand as if he were a child.

'Over by the wall there,' she pointed, 'were found two deep footprints. They were his - the animal. He must have jumped down there because the prints were so deep, well that's what someone told me anyway. Here by the lake' - her arm swept over to a point near the continuation of the copse – 'were many footprints indicating a struggle.'

Paul looked across the lake as if he expected to see them.

'They are gone now of course but I remember seeing them. The policeman pointed them out to me. I remember how cleverly he explained how the struggle must have been. I remember mother's neck, too, as she lay in bed. I expected it to be brown but it was blue.'

She looked at Paul.

'Do you find this interesting?'

'How did he get into the house?' he asked, ignoring the question.

'Why, he never left the grounds. There were footsteps to show that he had entered but none to show that he ever left.'

'So he must have waited until the following day to poison her.'

'Yes, she was poisoned.'

The woman stood out from the trees and looked across to the house. 'There is only me to carry on the honour of a great family.'

She paused.

'We have kept the family so close you know. Mother was father's cousin. They even looked alike. We have all looked alike since the seventeenth century.'

'All beautiful. All the ladies.'

It was Paul who had spoken. She turned to him as if she had forgotten he was there.

'Poor Paul,' she said, 'I am either maudlin or cruel. What do you think of me?'

Paul's expression indicated that her present kindness had swept away any other mood. Again he placed his hand in hers, not as a lover does but in the manner of a child. Again he followed where she led.

'I must show you more attention,' the woman said. 'You are very attentive to me and I am only cruel.'

As they walked back to the temple, he studied her face. One side of it was illuminated by the misty sunlight, the other was in shadow. She had never told him her age and it was impossible to guess it. She may have been thirty - even older, but hers was an ageless face, an adorable face.

She pushed open the door to the temple and he followed her inside. Again they sat on the stone bench seat.

'It is a strange story,' she said, 'and everyone believed it.'

'Why should they not?' he replied.

'Why not?' she laughed, 'Why...' She could not control her laughter. She was almost hysterical.

For a moment she calmed herself.

'The footprints,' she said, beginning again to smile, 'remember the footprints.'

'By the lake,' he said.

'Not by the lake. Not by the lake. The footprints which aren't there, the footprints which were never there. Do you know why he never left the park?'

'You told me. Because he waited.'

'He waited... he waited': She could barely speak for the laughter which seemed to control her.

'He waited,' she said again, 'at the bottom of the lake. He is still at the bottom of the lake!'

Paul looked up.

'Then she was avenged. They killed him,' he said.

'She was given her revenge on the animal - for being an animal. She killed him.'

'But...'

'She killed him by the lake. People would never believe she had such strength. But we all have it. All the "beautiful ladies" of this family have it. We all have our strength.'

'But she died.'

'By her own hand. They say she was insane. Absurd, but she was determined. She administered her own poison. She told me - she told me it all!'

She had been speaking at great speed. The truth was only slowly dawning on Paul. For a moment his companion was quiet, then she said:

'She told me. She had rid the world of an animal. She had played with him and dispensed with him. It was I who obtained the poison for her - I!'

Then she began to laugh. Paul had never seen her like this before. She rose before him like an avenging angel and blocked the weak sunlight from the window. As she moved towards the door her laughter became unbearable. Paul clapped his hands to his ears and could only watch her figure standing there; as her body shook with maniacal laughter and her hand felt for an object in the breast of her dress, as her other hand moved towards the door and turned the key in the lock.

The Christmas Horse

I stood at the bedroom window, watching the falling snow, black against the night, forming a bank against the cill. My wife slept and there was silence from my daughter's room. I sat on the side of the bed, unable to sleep. The small footsteps continued. That steady tread.

I rose unsteadily and walked out onto the landing. I followed the sound but could see nothing. I reached the nursery and turned the handle. It was stiff through lack of use but eventually it turned and I stepped apprehensively inside. The noise had stopped.

I shrugged and pulled the door to. Perhaps it was my imagination that I thought I could hear a rhythmic noise from the nursery as if something were moving backwards and forwards.

Backwards and forwards. Backwards and forwards.

Charlotte had always had imaginary companions - we left empty seats for them at table. For my daughter was an imaginative five year old and invented brothers, sisters and playmates with whom she would talk and play.

So we were unsurprised when Robin arrived, unannounced and - of course - unseen. I had little time to spare on the newcomer; the large newly acquired Victorian house in which we lived demanded most of my spare time, and the nursery was in the greatest need of renovation.

It was as I made a detailed search of this room that I discovered the rocking horse. I remember idly pushing it and the stiff squeaking noise it made - a noise which I clearly recalled. A noise which was repeated each time I pushed it. Backwards and forwards.

Backwards and forwards.

My daughter's laughter recalled me to the present and I blew the dust from the window and forced it open. There in the garden was Charlotte playing with her imaginary companion. From somewhere they had obtained a hoop and were bowling it with a stick around the garden. They? I laughed. Charlotte was quite alone.

When Christmas came it followed almost a month of sleepless nights spent listening. Listening to rhythmic child-like steps on the stairs. And on Christmas morning something drew me again to the old nursery. But when I visited it I saw a room which was completely different from the derelict dusty place I had previously seen. It was not just the decorations and discarded Christmas wrapping paper which lay on the floor. The room now resembled a Victorian playroom, and in it sat a sailor-suited boy with long curly locks. He was riding a rocking horse, similar to the one I had found, but seemingly brand new.

I left the room to look for my daughter. She in turn was looking for her imaginary playmate, but neither of us was ever to see him again.

Felicity

A man held a small red book before him and stared intently at the grey walls of Torre Abbey, constantly referring back to the book as if it acted as a guide to the building's stonework. Golfers from the adjoining golf course watched him, wiping the sweat from their faces as they walked to the next tee.

He had been observed for the past week; every day he held his little red book and every day examined the stones. But on this day he showed more activity than usual. His mournful face lit up with a smile and the book fell from his hand in a moment of excitement. He dropped to his knees and began to scoop away the earth and moss from the stone. Then he leaned back and surveyed the piece of excavated stone with great satisfaction. He retrieved his book and glanced at it again, then at the stone and gently closed the book as a minister would close a Bible.

A row of old ladies, who had missed none of this, watched two men in working clothes join the man with the book. For a moment the workmen stood, looking down, then one of them spoke:

'Very ancient them.'

Edwin Leary looked up.

'I beg your pardon? Oh yes, the walls. Yes very ancient. If only I had found them sooner.'

'Yer could have asked in the town.'

'No, no, I'm sorry. I was not referring to the abbey. I was thinking of these initials in the stonework.'

'Oh, them initials.'

'Yes. But it is no business of yours.'

'No business of mine! This abbey's my business. I was give this job whin I give up lookin' after the Tower of London 'cos it was known as I wanted a job down 'ere.'

'Please don't misunderstand me,' said Leary, pointing to the initials. 'The abbey is naturally your business, but these initials are mine. My business, and my initials too in fact,' he laughed.

'There's an L.'

'Yes, and an E. The initials are E. L..'

'I don't see any E.L..'

'Well it is a little difficult to decipher, I grant you, but, chipped as it is, I think there is no doubt that it is E.L.'

The workman laughed.

'Shall we tell 'im?' he said to his mate, a man of about twenty.

Leary looked up.

'Tell me what?'

'That them's ancient marks. Bin 'ere since the abbey were built. It's a mark what the builders put to show as they'd finished a section. And it ain't E. L.; the initials ain't yourn; it's a buildin' sign.'

The older workman put his bag over his back and walked off grinning to himself. Edwin Leary watched him go and noticed that his companion did not share his mirth.

Leary took his red book to a seat but soon the noise of its other occupants became too much for him, and he seated himself on the grass in the abbey grounds. He opened the book to the entry for the 29th June 1962 and read again the familiar words:

'Received Felicity's letter. She says she has carved my initials in the stone wall at Torre Abbey. "It is not easily found," she says, "it is not an act of desecration but an act of love".'

He closed the little red book and thought of what the workman had said. Then a shadow was cast across him.

'So it's a diary.' It was the younger workman.

'Yes,' replied Leary, 'it is a diary.'

'May I look?'

Leary looked up but did not proffer the diary.

'It was a joke you know,' the workman said.

'A joke? What was a joke?'

'Those are her initials I mean - not a building mark; that was Jack's joke about the building mark. Torre Abbey doesn't have them.'

'They are my initials.'

'Yes your initials - carved by her. The girl in the white dress. I don't like Jack's jokes. If you've come back after all this time you ought to know that I saw her writing those initials.'

'But you must have been...?'

'Ten. I was ten. Do you believe that a boy of ten could give up his life for a woman? If you don't, you cannot understand the type of man I am. I could have died for her.'

Leary handed him the diary and the workman stood reading it, pausing at intervals to brush the hair from his eyes. He handed back the diary without speaking and lowered himself to the grass.

'I used to come to the abbey every day when I was a boy. I used to come straight from school in the summer and lie on the grass. If I had homework to do I'd bring my satchel here and work, here on the grass. If I didn't have to work I'd come here and watch the people: it didn't matter, I was interested in people and I never got bored. I saw her first in June.'

'June the first?'

'Yes. June the first. I kept a diary too. I used to wonder why she always walked here alone.'

'Do you still wonder?'

'What happened in May? Or was it before May?'

'No, it was May. Please understand me, I would like to tell you more, but – it is difficult for me. You see I have a responsible position.'

The workman drew a forearm across his forehead and sat staring at the sweat which had collected on his arm. He appeared not to have been offended by Leary's reticence but nodded and returned to his story.

'Whatever happened in May,' he said, looking at Leary, 'June was a beautiful month and I came to look forward to my visits to the abbey. I even left school early to come here. And she was always here and always on her own. Then one day at the end of June - it was today ten years ago - I watched her scrabbling in the earth. She was there for some time and every few moments she would look over her shoulder to see if she were watched. But no one had seen her except me and I was lying under that tree (he pointed to the spot) and it would have been difficult for her to know that I had seen her. After that she replaced a few turfs and, with one last look around, she walked away down towards the front.'

'And did you look at what she had carved?' asked Leary.

'Of course. It would have been impossible for a ten year old boy to have done otherwise. I saw the letters that you saw, E. L..'

'And what did you think about them?'

'I thought they were the initials of the luckiest man alive.'

Leary laughed dryly. The workman continued.

'I couldn't get rid of the idea that they stood for Edward Lear. I was not so very wrong.'

'You are an observant young man. You got my name from the cover of my diary I suppose?'

The workman nodded and wiped his forehead again.

'Do you smoke?' he said proffering a packet of cigarettes.

Leary took one and, for some moments, they smoked in silence. Then the workman eased himself into a lying position and stared up at the sky.

'I am surprised you do not want to know where she is.'

'Oh I know.'

'Then... what do you know?'

'I know that she has not waited ten years for me. She must have married and...'

'No, you are wrong about that. She never married.'

'Then she lived with someone?'

The workman became angry.

'She lived with no one. She walked alone and she lived alone. And she had only one friend.'

'One friend?'

'I was eleven then. When I spoke to her.'

'Oh, I see. I am sorry. Then I must see her.'

'I will take you on one condition.'

'Do you presume to make conditions?' Leary said angrily.

'You did not come from London - and I know you came from London - merely to see those initials. They were important, I know, for if they had never been written...'

'Alright. What are your conditions?'

'I said one condition. I ask only one return for my information. I loved her with the platonic love of a boy; I placed her on a pedestal. I dreamed of her and, as I said, I would have died for her. But that kind of love changes with time.'

'You mean you...'

'E.L. never came,' he continued, ignoring Leary's interruption, 'and she was still young. There was no need for her to always walk alone - and I wanted her. I was sixteen when I began to join her on her walks.'

'And you...?'

Walked with her. Only walked with her. Why are you so worried about me? You were ready to give her up to a stranger...'

'But you are not a stranger now and you are beginning to shame me. I am sorry.'

'What happened on your walks?'

'We talked. Not of you,' he said hurriedly, noticing Leary's glance. 'We talked of the abbey and of the people who come to sit here every day. And… and one day I put my arm around her, but she smiled sadly and removed it. She said she was waiting for someone. She often spoke like that - and of what would happen when that someone returned to her.'

Leary extinguished his cigarette on the sole of his boot and threw it onto the grass.

'I have to clear that up,' said the workman, picking up the end and throwing it into a bin, 'and she is the reason for my working here.'

'You mean you...?'

'Threw up the chance of a university place, threw up everything - angered my parents, annoyed my school teachers, and took a job in the abbey. This was the only job they had for me.'

Leary rose to his feet and extended an arm to help the workman to his feet. 'And now you must take me to her.'

'On that one condition. I told you so much because you may not otherwise have agreed to my condition. She would tell me nothing. Why did she have to wait for you?' Leary pulled out his diary and handed it to the workman.

'It's in there,' he said.

He handed back the diary without looking at it.

'I want it from you,' he said.

Leary put the diary in his pocket and ran a hand over his forehead to collect the sweat.

You know her name of course. Felicity. Perhaps you didn't know that she was born here in Devon?'

'She told me that. But go on.'

'She came to London when she was sixteen, and I was twenty four when I met her. Perhaps this doesn't matter?'

'I should like to hear it.'

'Well, she was an attractive girl - you know that. And she...'

'Attracted you?'

'Yes.' Leary looked down at his feet as he walked. 'Yes she attracted me and I... well she was beautiful and you must know how difficult it is to...'

'I know how difficult. I have only touched her that once and I have never held her hand. Never...' His voice tailed off and Leary looked at him for the first time with sympathy.

'Well, I was in business,' he continued, 'and I had given up all aspirations to join the church. Yes it must sound strange, but my father was a vicar and, in many ways, he reminded me of a Puritan. When I told him that Felicity was with child he threatened to turn me out of the house and the family business if I did not send her away.'

'And you chose the business?'

'Please try to understand. I ask you to put yourself in my position - a young man with every opportunity before him.'

He looked at the workman and then at the sun. The sun was hot on his forehead and he moved over to walk in the shade. 'Anyway I was forced to leave her.'

'She left you,' the workman corrected.

'Well, she went away and... and had the baby.'

'Which you paid for.'

'I sent money. Oh yes, I stood by her. Please don't believe that I just left her. I sent her money and sometimes even food from the shop - when I say shop, it was a chain of shops - and then she came back. She came back at the end of May and, by then, the child was a few months old. Of course I couldn't let my father see her or the child. So she offered - offered mind you - to go away to some friends who lived in Devon.'

'She had no friends here.'

'No, it appears not. But she went away and she said she would come back when she had settled the child somewhere.' He looked at the workman. 'Do you know what happened to the child?'

'Yes. She kept it here. She told me. But someone came to see her. I never knew who it was but I think I know now. The child went away - perhaps to stay with a relation.'

'She had no relations.'

'Anyway, the child went away.'

'And who was her visitor?'

'I don't know. He wore a clerical collar. I don't know any more than that.'

Leary kicked a stone. They had reached the churchyard. The workman held open the gate and their feet made crunching noises on the gravel path.

'I must see the child,' Leary said. 'Father had no right to do what he did. I must help the child. I don't care now about the business as long as I can make it happy.'

The workman had stopped and was pointing to a white grave-stone.

'There is Felicity,' he said.

Remembering The Fifth

I watched as the days shortened and the air took on that autumnal scent redolent of bonfires and crackling leaves. As my father and I walked through the park gates, the brown brittle leaves crackled under our feet and the breath of the boys playing football showed smoke white against the cold air. We would watch the match at Ilford and return through the park but for once the talk was not all of football and which blue and white hoop shirted hero had scored for the 'Ford. There was talk also of Guy Fawkes' Night and of those gaily coloured fireworks which lurked at home, even the smallest modestly hiding its moments of glory in a small insignificant case.

And when my father said: 'Well, I'm not going to see them again' (as he always did when Ilford lost or played badly), it was about as significant a statement as if he had said 'There will be no Guy Fawkes this year'. Somehow the two would always be there, just as my father would always be an omnipotent god and the world a vast place of mystery. After all Guy Fawkes had been there since late September, staring from the window bills in shop windows, advising us to be wise and buy a certain brand of firework. We ignored him: we must get some of everything; I wished I could buy every firework there was.

This year the invitations were being made as October made her blustery entry into the calendar - uncles, aunts, friends. I chose in those days to minimise the efforts of my mother, slaving in the kitchen to ensure that cold hands could be clasped round hot cups of soup before, hungry and cold, they could attack the bangers, spuds in jackets, chicken and flapjacks. Somehow food was not important then and I preferred not to think of the time when the last firework had died and the glowing, pulsating, exciting evening was dark once more. But if my mother's important role did not receive the approbation from me which it richly deserved, the part to be played by my Uncle Will was appreciated fully.

Everyone should have an Uncle Will, indeed I thought then

that everyone did have one. It was like having a father and mother; I assumed they were compulsory. And my Uncle Will was everything an Uncle Will should be. He told fascinating tales which seemed to improve with every telling. And his life seemed larger than the life of ordinary folk.

I had no way of knowing then that his stories *did* improve with every telling, that his remarkable imagination built them from a core of truth until the original was lost or distorted. But no one could deny that his had been an exciting life and that his job as a London cabby had provided him with a fund of fascinating material.

His naval career - he had served with great honour in the First World War - had left him with two things. A collection of tattoos and a hand shake that rattled his cup in its saucer when he picked up his tea to drink. The tattoos were a work of art, and the one he was proudest of showing proclaimed loudly 'Mary'. And indeed it was to Mary, my mother's sister, that he had shown a consistent devotion throughout his adult life.

In the second war, too old for service, he had used his considerable courage as an A.R.P. warden and this left him with an arsenal of thunderflashes and smoke bombs which he stored in his shed. It was the smoke bomb that caused all the trouble.

Uncle Will was proud of his garden and I used to watch him dig and weed it and share his breaks in the garden shed. He showed me his arsenal in early September during one such break. The thunderflashes looked innocuous - white 'bangers' with red writing and pink touch paper. The smoke bomb was a large brooding monster.

'We'll try a few of them on Guy Fawkes' Night, boy,' he promised. But my Aunt Mary had appeared and talk on this subject ceased.

He spoke instead about the processions he had witnessed in the East End of London at a time when families of the district were too poor to buy their own fireworks. He described the Guy Fawkes processions in vivid detail - led by a giant figure whose construction had taken many months and whose origins owed more to the Green Man than to Guy Fawkes.

When Saturday - the Fifth of November - arrived, I approached the coming evening in a state of uncontrollable excitement. The morning had been spent in performing the usual - delightful - Guy Fawkes tasks. The filling of buckets with earth - and one with water; the sinking of rocket-launching tubes, the cleaning down of the old iron table for small fountains and cones and - best of all - the pinning on of Catherine wheels. My father used a large piece of trellis and he would allow me to arrange the wheels on the trellis.

There was Flying Scotsman, Devil's Grindstone, Flaming Flywheel, Spider's Webb and the colours matched the imagination of the names.

But the greatest magic of all was when the first touch paper was lit and began to sizzle. It heralded a wonderful evening of jumping crackers, rockets, gerbes, squibs and flying dragons. We were dazzled by snow storms and shimmering cascades and excited by air bombs and screechers. The darkness was lit with electric brightness by the rising stars from Roman candles - and the noise of bangers and the crackles of crackpots broke the eerie stillness of the night.

My Uncle Will had been suspiciously quiet throughout. His excursion to 'light a banger' was his first venture into the darkness. But the noise that 'the banger' made was not to be forgotten by the onlookers. I recalled our talk in his garden shed and remembered the thunderflashes. My ears told me that I had just heard one.

We certainly had the loudest bangers that year but, carefully planned by Uncle Will, we had not yet seen all he could do. As the finale saxon started spinning we noticed his absence and expected the noise of another thunderflash. Instead of this a blanket of smoke approached us from the end of the garden. As cold hands were clapped together and feet stamped to get warmth into cold limbs the saxon produced its last sparks, its case spinning darkly round on its nail like a rusty wheel. But the fog thickened.

The party gathered indoors but the fog penetrated the open windows and filled the rooms with smoke.

Windows were hastily closed and the door slammed on the last guest as he entered the house. But it was a long time before that smoke cleared. And, although no evidence was ever found of it, there was little doubt in my mind that I had seen a monster war time smoke bomb in action.

What To Make of Delia

I wondered what had brought me there. Dreams? Dreams of Delia as she had been? Or revenge? Perhaps I really thought I could exact revenge for her rejection of me. I looked around at the large featureless room. Once it had been a Victorian's sitting room. He and his family would have sat at a long oak table and talked quietly while servants bustled and the world waited.

But now nothing of that remained except a damaged crystal chandelier hanging at a slight angle from the ceiling. Its presence could not evoke the room's past.

'You have noticed the chandelier?' Delia asked.

I nodded. I had. It was superb.

'It is broken,' Delia amended.

'Broken yes,' I murmured, 'Once it must have been lovely.'

Delia looked at me as if I had sidestepped a blow. She, too, wondered what had brought me here and I was expected to provide an answer to her unstated question.

'I wondered what had happened to you,' I said lamely.

Delia smiled without humour.

'Well now you see,' she said.

I had seen and it had given me no pleasure. To see a woman whose hair had once shone in the sun and created a golden storm in the breeze. To see her defeated, ignoble, wearing a torn dress, her hair arranged like that of a washerwoman. That could give no satisfaction.

I thrust my hands into my pockets, seeking an opportunity to leave. Delia picked up an iron and resumed the work my arrival had interrupted. It was as if to indicate that her time was more precious than mine, even if her tasks were more mundane.

'Do you ever think of Berkeley?' I asked.

'Berkeley?'

I pulled out my pipe. I felt better with it in my hand. For a few moments I filled and lit it.

'Berkeley?' she queried again in a flat voice.

I drew on the pipe and exhaled.

'You must remember Berkeley,' I replied.

Her lack of response and the continued ardour of the ironing indicated that she did not remember.

'I took you to Berkeley,' I said lamely.

She waved away the pipe smoke and pointed to the window. My eyes followed her direction.

'Would you open the window?' she said.

'Oh! My pipe. I'm sorry. If you'd prefer I didn't ...'

'It will be alright if you open the window.'

I opened the window and replaced the pipe in my pocket. Again I felt ill at ease.

'You were saying,' she said, 'that you took me to Berkeley. I don't remember. Where is Berkeley?'

Absurdly I could not remember.

'Somewhere near your home. Somewhere near Cheltenham.'

'Berkeley Castle,' she said suddenly, something of the old gleam returning to her eyes. 'Of course I went to the castle - was it with you?'

I did not reply because that moment's elation had changed Delia. It had taken away her iron, her ironing board; it had dressed her in a short blue and white summer frock and spread that tied up hair into a profusion of golden ringlets. Once more she smiled that tantalising smile and her hands were white and smooth again.

I had seen that the old Delia still existed underneath her drab suburban mask. And I realised now why I had come. Revenge was too strong a word for it. I suppose I could describe it as a desire to be her equal. I wished, with my new found position, to make the old vivacious Delia laugh with me instead of at me; to make her consider me a person rather than another suitor of which she had had so many. Also I wished to understand her.

Having seen Delia smile in remembrance suggested to me that there was some pleasure in recollection and that made me feel better. As we talked of things that could not animate us, I thought of the past that Delia's smile had brought back. I was not to know why the memory of Berkeley had affected her so.

Her mother held a cup of tea towards me.

'There you are my dear. You like it strong?'

I looked at the thick brown tea.

I said that I did like it strong.

Delia came back from collecting the picnic basket and deposited it on the floor.

'Oh, Mamma, You've made him tea. You didn't have to. It wasn't necessary.'

Her mother smiled but said nothing.

'We are going to Berkeley,' Delia said.

Her mother smiled:

'Where your father took me,' she said.

'I don't remember,' said Delia.

'It was where he proposed to me, my dear.'

Delia looked shaken. The thought had disconcerted her and she stared at me in a threatening way as if I had chosen the spot for its significance.

'Well, that won't happen to us, Mamma.'

Her mother smiled at me like a conspirator.

'Of course, of course,' she said. 'You are too young.'

But Delia was not too young and her mother was well aware of it.

I relaxed into my chair and sipped my tea. The sun cast patterns of lace over the room and a slight breeze ruffled the curtains. I was content. I could smell Delia's perfume and considered it a compliment to me.

'And bring her home in time for the last 'bus from the square...' her mother was saying.

'Oh, Mamma, he will not be bringing me home. He is not taking me; I am going with him. And I will be returning on my own; he has to get back to Bristol.'

Her mother frowned.

'But, my dear...'

Whatever remonstrance she had intended to make went unsaid. Delia had left the room in search of a quite unnecessary umbrella.

The 'bus arrived at Berkeley at ten. Delia had kept up a constant stream of excited conversation throughout the journey but, to my chagrin, had indicated by her talk that I was less her young man than a companion whose sex she had not noticed.

Much of her babbling had required no reply and I had been able, without being noticed, to study her closely. Her body had brushed against mine every time the 'bus lurched or turned. Her decorous attempts to move away from the moments of contact had usually been frustrated by my less obvious moves to engineer them.

As we left the 'bus Delia stopped, turned to me and said:

'Did you have the feeling you were being vetted?'

'Vetted? By whom?'

'By my Mamma.' Then she laughed - loudly - at the absurdity of it all.

I was pleased. Absurd as it might have been, it made me feel - considered. I counted to someone, even if only someone so out of touch with Delia's true feelings.

I was gratified too that Delia had chosen to mention it, although I realised it was an offering that would only too soon be swept away in the laughter of derision. Delia led me on, perhaps unintentionally, with these offerings, for she must have known that I loved her and that the laughter hurt.

Our tour of the castle was not a success. I had taken her hand and she had not withdrawn it as she had on previous occasions. But she had broken away in an excess of enthusiasm for an objet d'art which had evaporated once our hands were disengaged. Thereafter her hands were always occupied - carrying the picnic basket, unnecessarily, in two hands or holding the hand of an obnoxious child who had strayed from its parent and thoroughly deserved to be lost.

Delia delighted in talking to everyone. She flattered old men, expressing amazement at their youthfulness and fondled cats with an enthusiasm which caused me to envy them. She sat on chairs which bore unmistakable notices forbidding it. But, somehow, she got away with it. Delia always did.

I tried to impress her with my knowledge of history. I recounted the events leading up to the murder of Edward II but she was not listening. She would say: 'Oh, what a lot you know,' in a tone which suggested that I knew very little. I can remember so clearly the picnic lunch which we ate and my pleasure at the knowledge that she had prepared it herself.

As she poured the tea from a vacuum flask I watched her curls fall about her shoulders and the hem of her dress ride dangerously high over her thighs. I resisted the temptation to touch the expanse of smooth skin thus revealed; it would have been an action to prevent any further enjoyment of the day.

I wanted the meal to last for ever; I tried to prolong it by lying out in the hot August sun but Delia would not join me. She covered her head to protect herself from the sun and seemed determined that her soft white skin should not meet its rays.

'My family has a connection with Berkeley,' she said suddenly.

'Yes your father. He proposed...'

'Oh, you cannot forget that can you?' she said and laughed. 'I wonder whether Mamma made it up?'

I smiled. 'I see no reason...'

But she ignored me.

'My family have an important connection with Berkeley. The abbot here - you know the abbey.'

I shook my head.

'We are walking towards it,' she said. 'Quite by coincidence.'

She laughed again and indicated a low church which had none of the grandeur that its name indicated.

I asked which abbot provided the connection.

'Abbot Tunwell. He was on my father's side.'

'That would have been...?'

'A long time ago,' she laughed. 'I haven't your talent with dates. He was a brother of my great great grandfather.'

'About a hundred years ago - about eighteen sixty?' I asked.

'I'm sure you're right,' she said. 'They go a long way back.'

She paused as if deep in thought.

'There are still Tunwells,' she said. 'But we don't get on. They're an odd family - like us,' she added.

We had reached a low wall from which I jumped. There was a drop of several feet and I held up my hand to help her down.

'Oh no,' she said as if my offer were made entirely for the pleasure that the contact with her would bring.

Instead she leapt, her ankle turned, and she stood as if in pain.

I offered assistance, kneeling to look at the ankle, but as I did so she walked off, not without a slight limp but with little indication of the pain she had apparently felt.

Suddenly I was angry. I talked about the abbey and walked briskly, knowing it would hurt her to keep to my pace.

The abbey, by now, was bathed in an orange glow cast by the lowering sun. The soft coloured stone radiated a warmth which neither of us can have felt. The interior of the building was no different to that of a medium sized church. Delia picked up a guide to the history of the building and handed it to me.

'Tell me about the abbey. I have never known anything about it,' she said.

The teasing tone had gone. She looked at a picture of the abbey as I read from the guide and, as I spoke softly, I turned my face towards hers and she, to hear, bent her head a little so that her face was nearly touching mine. At intervals she would ask for elucidation of certain architectural descriptions; at others she would ask which reign a certain event had happened in. She liked to keep the history 'in perspective'.

I could smell her perfume. Once her cheek brushed against mine and, although she nervously withdrew her face, she had smiled.

Before I had finished reading the guide she sat down at a pew and motioned for me to do the same. I stopped reading and sat at her side. She placed a finger to her lips and concentrated on the music of the abbey's organ which was playing as if by appointment.

'It is so lovely. So peaceful.'

For some minutes we sat listening. Then she leapt up.

'There is a staircase,' she said. 'It leads to the rood screen.'

I looked up. There was no rood screen.

'You read it to me,' she said. 'Let's find it.'

I looked back over what I had read but knew that there had been no mention of a rood screen. For the first time I doubted the sincerity of her mood. Did she indeed know the abbey's history? Was she being kind in listening to my explanations, or was she mocking me?

Delia was by now climbing the spiral staircase to which she had referred and which had originally afforded an entry point to a long forgotten rood screen.

'It is lovely here too,' she said. 'You can see the whole nave. It seems so far down.'

She was just talking, as she often did. She had a delightful voice; it was unimportant that what she said was of little account. She edged to one side to let me see down into the body of the church. To do so my body came closer to hers than it had ever done. Her look told me that she was not unaware of this and her kindly attitude toward me vanished.

'I wonder how many people have committed suicide from here?' she said.

I noticed the angle of her body as she leaned over the low barrier. There was no sense in what she said. Unless it was that suicide was preferable to contact with me. I could not rid myself of the idea that she was mocking me again.

Suddenly she bent forward. I caught her arm but she did not attempt to jump. She shrugged me off contemptuously.

'If you would like to go down I can follow,' she said archly.

I shrugged and descended the staircase.

The strains of the organ were still in our ears as we issued again into the cool evening air. The sun's red semi circle was visible over the castle giving that building and the surrounding park an orange aspect which emphasised both their age and gentility.

The bus waited in the market square. I remember Delia's face as we parted, smiling as if I were an acquaintance to whom politeness was necessary.

She was smiling that same smile as the sun descended on the less aesthetic buildings opposite her present home.

I was conscious of the pipe in my hand, of Delia waiting for a reply. I started:

'I'm sorry. I was thinking of...'

'Of what?'

'I was thinking of Berkeley. I am surprised it does not mean more to you. It meant a great deal to me.'

Delia put down her iron.

'That surprises me now as much as it would have surprised me

170

then. And I'm afraid I still doubt it.'

I protested.

'Then I believe you,' she said. 'I cannot do otherwise. But your presence here is hard to explain. I do not think you came purely to talk of old times to a woman whose marriage has made her station in life different from your own.'

I toyed with my pipe. I was unsure how it had come to be in my hands again.

'I wish only that you would not underestimate my feelings,' I stammered. 'I-I don't know why I came here. I didn't know what I would find.'

'I do not underestimate them; I do not think that I overestimate them either. I think I have never known you better.'

I looked up puzzled.

'My husband will be home soon,' she said. 'If you would like to meet him...?'

'No, I... I don't think so.'

'He knows of Berkeley too. It is strange.'

'But you said you had forgotten Berkeley until I...'

'He knows of Berkeley too,' she repeated, ignoring my interruption. 'He once showed me a spiral staircase at the abbey. I remember he had an obsession with that staircase - he thought that it would be an ideal place to die. He had strange thoughts, I used to think. But he was interesting. He intrigued me. I felt that he would not read history. He would make history.'

I looked at Delia's shabby surroundings and felt for my matches.

'I must go,' I said.

'You would not like to meet him?'

I shook my head.

'And yet he is so much a part of your dream of Berkeley.'

Again I shook my head. No I did not want to meet him. Delia followed me into the hall. After I had left the house I paused to light my pipe. As I waited I saw a man enter the house. He was dressed smartly in a suit and carried a brief case. It was only then that I realised that the interior of the house could alter so much according to its occupant. Instead of the piles of ironing, the ironing board and the woman Delia had become, I imagined a table laid for dinner and this man, seated, waiting for his meal.

I started to walk back to the station with Delia's words ringing in my ears. The annoyance was that still I did not know what to make of Delia.

If The Truth Were Known

It was a long time before I discovered who was responsible for the pictures at the allotments.

I used to help my cousin on his allotment when I was a youngster - doing the sort of job that, as an adult, I should find tedious. I should like to have such a boy to help me now as I toil at the raspberry canes and overgrown jungle which were once a neat garden plot. But I have become used to being alone, and it was no different when I was a boy. The company of my cousin, welcome as it was, was secondary to my love of taking on and succeeding in a job that others were unprepared to tackle.

It was as I heaved a large stone from the overgrown plot which would soon be, thanks to our efforts, a neat and respectable allotment that I saw the first picture.

I dropped the stone heavily and then stooped to retrieve it as if I had dropped it on a small creature. When I rolled it back the momentary impression was confirmed. A face smiled at me as though in gratitude for having the weight removed. But then its smile changed as the paper on which it was printed relaxed from the removal of the weight. The smile encouraged, enticed. Had I not been certain that the paper had no life of its own I should have said it beckoned to me.

I let the stone fall back a few feet from the picture and looked round for my cousin. He was working on, pausing every few moments only to relight his pipe.

I kept him in my sight while stooping to pick up the photograph. It had been partly hidden in the earth and I sat on my haunches keeping a wary eye on my cousin - ready to busy myself with some unnecessary task to cover the embarrassment of my discovery.

I brushed the earth from the photograph with all the care of an archaeologist removing the encrustations of age from a long hidden relic. And then its transference from the earth to my inside pocket was the work of a moment.

As I made my way back to where my cousin was working the photograph made a rustling noise in my pocket. To me it seemed that it must be possible to hear it in the road several hundred yards away, but my cousin seemed not to notice it.

I performed a few perfunctory tasks and then looked for more stones to clear. The clearance of the allotment had now become secondary to entering the little copse where I had discovered the photograph.

I took five stones to it before discovering another photograph. I had almost decided that the one which nestled against my breast was the only one, when another glint of colour caught my eye. I rushed to it, remembered, retrieved the stone I was carrying and deposited it beside the new photograph. The sight that met my eye on this occasion was enough to make me dangerously unaware of my cousin's presence. When I had looked at the part of a female body which I had never before dreamt existed - let alone seen, I had been transfixed by it. Revolted at first. By degrees interested, fascinated and enthralled. Could it be that women looked like this under their... I caught the gaze of my cousin in my direction just in time.

I straightened as if from a back breaking job; stooped again and moved the stone so it covered the photograph, fondling a weed as I did so as if I had saved it from destruction.

As I returned to my cousin I looked in his direction. He was back at work. I was unsure when he had turned away, but knew that my reaction had been the right one. I must leave the search for new photographs or I should be discovered and the objects of my search destroyed.

No doubt I had behaved in a most guilty fashion for the rest of that day. No doubt, too, my cousin had recognised that my increased efforts in the allotment round him were the result of a desire to be elsewhere rather than of my usual capacity for hard work.

However he said nothing as I should say nothing now about any young relative of mine. I wondered then what he would have said - and thought - had he known, but - in retrospect - I think he would still have done as he did.

I had to wait a week until I could return to the allotment. And then it was by telling the first lie I can ever remember telling my parents. I said I was going to do some work on my cousin's allotment - and hoped that I should be able to do some to justify my story.

In the event I did none for the discovery I made required such detailed planning that work was out of the question.

My discovery was not made immediately. It took a careful search until isolated finds led me to a place deep in the copse where a considerable number of torn photographs had been discarded.

More interesting was a pile at its centre: here the photographs were neatly stacked, tied, and - to the libidinous joy of their discoverer - not mutilated.

I picked up the pile and, under it, was another and - stacked against a tree - a further five or six bundles.

At first my hands trembled so much I was unable to untie the string but eventually a pile of coloured photographs of a young and very attractive lady lay loose in my lap. I flicked over them quickly like a boy stuffing in as many chocolates as he could before discovery could deny him consumption of the remainder. For this was a furtive exercise of which I was deeply ashamed.

The one important thing about the young lady in the photographs was that she was naked. It seemed to me then that she was incredibly naked - as if she had discarded more clothes than she had ever possessed. Some heightened the effect by displaying a pile of those discarded clothes in a pile beside her. So recently they had encased that lovely body, had been thrown aside. Those stockings, those suspenders, those panties...

I had no plans to take these delicious evils home. I could not have faced my parents knowing them to be in my desk - where all my other private belongings reposed - far less risk the very real danger of their discovery.

The thought that they might be lost, damaged by the elements or discovered by one of the other allotment holders was uppermost in my mind. I wondered if I could risk leaving them there.

I decided I could not but that, largely sheltered by the trees, they were initially safe from damage by rain and that the weight of the bundles protected them at least from distribution by the wind.

My first task, then, was to collect any stray photographs and bundle them together - a task which would also prevent discovery of outlying finds leading to the main hoard.

For a few moments my pleasure in the pictures prevented the beginning of this operation and, when I had prepared myself for it, it became apparent that I had been saved from ignominious discovery.

Another allotment holder had started work on his plot and I decided that my clearing up operations must be confined to the immediate vicinity of the copse.

I kept a close eye on the allotments while moving round the area within a small radius from my main find and, in doing so, discovered another stack of photographs which I moved to the safety of the trees.

The weeks that followed were taken up with the more mundane tasks which life had allotted to me. I took my thoughts to school and dreamt of the girl in the photographs. Always she called to me from the allotments asking me to help her, protect her, and, as reward, she allowed me to see her as she was in the photos. I knew her better, I felt, than her photographer. To him she would have been just another model. For this reason it was somehow inevitable that I should meet her. And meet her I did.

I was passing the State Cinema on my way to school when I stopped, as I always did, to look at the stills outside. I probably knew more about recent films than most people although I never actually could afford to go inside the cinema. And there were usually plenty of pretty girls.

But on this occasion my attention was drawn from the stills to a girl standing by the entrance to the cinema. I hastily turned back to the pictures and was sure she had not seen me, but as I continued to stare at the stills I was actually looking at her reflection in the glass.

Having stared at one print for so long I deemed it wise to move on. But I did so in the knowledge - and my work at school suffered because of it - that I had stared at the living breathing original of the girl in the photographs.

My initial reaction was of disappointment. A girl in a photograph could be mine. A girl waiting for - I didn't know whom - at a cinema entrance was neither mine nor could ever be mine. She was clearly eighteen, nineteen... perhaps even older. Older than I was, probably, by nearly a decade. She had not recognised me as her ardent admirer nor, perhaps, noticed my existence. She would certainly not remember the boy who stared at her in the safety of a reflection.

I was enslaved by the girl in the photographs and was as unlikely to be released by her as I was to be recognised by her living original. But I began to smile at her when I saw her - and I saw her with increasing frequency standing outside the entrance to the cinema.

And I returned to the allotment. I had not been for a week but, during my previous visits, I had tidied up the area surrounding the copse so that all stray photographs had been rounded up and deposited with their more safely stacked counterparts. There was much still to do. The danger of discovery was very real despite my efforts, and removal to a safer place essential.

I have mentioned my reluctance to take the photographs home; my search for a suitable place to store them therefore involved a reconnaissance of the environs of the allotments. Eventually I discovered - or rediscovered for I had played there often - an air raid shelter which was eminently suitable for the purpose.

I armed myself with a torch and slid my body through the small slit that was all that remained of the shelter's entrance. Inside the smell was worse now than I remembered it and I nearly dismissed it out of hand. But as I wandered round, the suitability of the place for storage and concealment forced me to re-consider. It was ideal. I should have to adapt it.

Over the next few weeks I rendered the shelter a much more suitable hideaway. I removed the accumulated rubbish of many years and took an air freshener of my mother's into its depths. But what did more to render its stale smelling interior acceptable was my clearance of its blocked entrance and the admission of more fresh air. The greenery had solved the problems which might have been caused by the clearance - the shelter would only have been known to those who had actually used it or played there before nature had taken its course.

I was prepared for the fact that people might enter it - although anyone who had entered it recently before my renovation was unlikely to return - and against that eventuality I had constructed in one of the blocked areas a camouflaged entrance and an under floor cavity within the so formed 'room'. If in my nervous state I had considered it secure then, in retrospect, I should imagine it was completely so.

The day for moving my photographs dawned misty and dank. After I had arrived at the copse, drops of rain began to fall on the leaves of the trees. I waited for some time before deciding that the move must take place - rain or no rain.

I could hear the rain clearly from inside the shelter as I lifted the last sack from my shoulder ready for its concealment.

This was the work of a moment and the time had come to make the long awaited final inspection of the photographs. I removed the block which covered the hole in which I had deposited them and sat on a stool I had brought with me on a previous occasion.

The girl smiled at me as I relaxed against the wall of the shelter. She winked, enticed, undressed. She sat amongst a pile of her discarded under-garments. She gyrated to unheard music. She smiled - just for me, and I studied her smiling face for some time before leaving the shelter and braving the rain.

It was a relief to be able to make my journey to school each day knowing that I had saved the girl from the shame that discovery of the photographs would have brought. I had improved the facilities at the shelter - which I visited weekly - installing a liquid gas stove for brewing tea, and fitting up a battery powered light as a substitute for the torch. But, somehow, my belief in the girl was waning. How could I believe that she was really displaying her charms to me when she, in reality, seemed not to notice me when I passed?

I had no way of knowing whether she would have responded to a greeting since my smiles were deliberately ambiguous; they could have been the smiles of a boy at peace with the world or one suddenly remembering a pleasant thought. A better directed smile might have resulted in a turning of the girl's head or a frown - and such an obvious rejection I could in no way risk.

So my visits to the shelter lost some of their fascination. I had by now seen the pictures so many times that the erotic poses had lost their immediate charm. And I had almost decided that my visit to the shelter on a beautifully sunny afternoon would be my last.

However events determined that it should not be so. I had spent perhaps an hour in the shelter; I had even said goodbye to the girl when I left the shelter - with perhaps less caution than I should normally have felt necessary.

But what I saw then made me duck back into its entrance. It was a man in the copse in which I had originally found the photographs - a man in an attitude of one who is searching.

I waited for what seemed a long time - but was probably only a few minutes - for the man to leave the copse. But then, to my horror, I heard a step on the tangled undergrowth outside. I flattened myself against the wall but a shadow, cast across the entrance, suggested I had been discovered. It was useless to move further into the shelter where I should be trapped. My only hope was that the man would take a quick look inside and not notice me in the dark recesses of the entrance.

It was a forlorn hope. He pressed on and his hand grabbed my arm and pulled me forward.

'Who are you?'

I remained silent, staring at him in terror.

'Where are the photos?'

I should have denied knowledge of any photos. My hiding in an air raid shelter - surely something which a boy was likely to do - was no evidence of guilt in this regard. But I mumbled:

'I was... trying to help.'

'Ah! So you have moved them. I thought a kid wouldn't bolt back into his hole in that guilty fashion without there being some good reason for it.'

He looked at me closely, his head near to mine. Then he began to shake me and demand where the photographs were hidden.

My period of captivity was short lived. There was no point in the man's threats of violence. He was clearly not strong and he must have realised that any violent act would have increased the likelihood of my inform-ing. However I considered that I had not been entirely innocent in the affair and this would have made any report to the authorities a difficult one to make without self incrimination.

I decided to play down my role in the affair. He was clearly badly frightened and was not thinking clearly enough to establish the reasons for my moving the photographs - reasons I had no intention of divulging for, while I held the trump card, another idea was forming in my mind.

'I won't tell.'

'You'd better not because I'll...'

'Do nothing. I don't think you can. And I know all about you.'

Here I was on difficult ground. A mistake here could jeopardise a plan that was becoming increasingly important to me.

'You are a photographer.' I tried to conceal my apprehension but to my inestimable relief he looked further discomfited and showed by his reaction that my guess had been correct. 'You are a photographer and your model waits outside the State Cinema every Tuesday and Thursday.'

I had done enough. I had implied that she waited for him without stating it.

But it was clearly true. He mumbled:

'I... She is a nice girl, I... You are thinking wrong things. It was purely that...' His words died out as he turned upon me again in anger:

'What are you going to do?'

I appeared to consider, then stated with a confidence I did not entirely feel:

'It depends.'

'Depends on what?'

I had to choose my words carefully.

'I should like to see how they're done... photo sessions. If I could see one...'

'Dirty little creep.'

I decided to curtail my justified protest.

'You just want to see her... You want to see. Well you won't be able to. I don't see her now. It was wise that we... that there were no more photos.'

'And you don't see her for any other reason?'

'No!'

'Then it's a pity.' I shook my head sorrowfully.

'What do you mean?'

'Well my clear duty...'

'Is to keep quiet. Is to keep quiet. To keep your grubby little hands out of my business.'

I started to walk out of the shelter.

'Where are you going?'

'Home.'

'No you're not. I haven't finished with you.'

'I'm going home.'

He grabbed my shoulder and flung me against the wall. Again my words belied my feelings:

'If you hit me, I'll tell the police.'

'And if I don't?'

'I'll tell my Dad and let him decide what to do.'

He smiled. Thank the good Lord, he had smiled.

'So I have a chance if you tell your Dad. He might do nothing?'

I shrugged.

He leaned wearily against the wall.

'When do you want to see her? I assume you don't really want to see me photographing her?'

I shrugged again. It was becoming a habit.

'I'll see if she'll... do what she did in the photos. And then you won't do anything?'

'Nothing,' I said eagerly.

And, as I walked out into the blazing sunshine, it was with the light tread of one who has gained a major victory and whose life had changed as a result of it. I had been totally unprepared for the man's question, 'Where shall it be?' I had never thought that I should actually meet the girl. But I had replied quickly enough: 'Next Wednesday. Here.' As if the chance would be gone if arrangements were not made quickly.

The following Wednesday was another blazing day. It seemed a good omen for I had wondered how willing a girl would be to strip in a dank shelter on a cool day. Doubts still assailed my mind and I don't think I really believed that she would actually be there.

It was therefore a surprise when I entered the shelter to find her sitting in the corner on a wooden box which had served as part of my seating arrangements.

I sat on another box and for a moment neither of us spoke. She was as lovely as I had ever seen her and, for once, the shelter smelled of perfume. I took it as a compliment to me that she had bothered with perfume.

Suddenly she said:

'Shall I start?'

I just stared.

She reached for the zip at the back of her dress and pulled it down; then, standing up, let the dress fall to her feet.

She was wearing a white slip with pink and green flowers along the border; she sat again, still not looking at me. She looked infinitely sad and I felt uncomfortable.

She pulled the straps of her slip over her arms and, again standing, wriggled until the garment fell to the floor.

I wondered why it was necessary for her to sit again. We were both distinctly embarrassed. The absurdity of the situation must have been apparent to both of us - a woman stripping in a fashion totally devoid of the erotic and a boy preferring to look elsewhere while she did so.

'Stop,' I said suddenly as she reached for the hook of her bra.

She looked at me disinterestedly as if stopping or continuing was immaterial to her.

She brought her hand to her lap, looking up at me for a direction I could not give. We looked at each other uneasily. It was the noise of a car that rescued us from the situation.

We both turned in alarm. There was no road. The girl walked quietly to the entrance of the shelter. She did not need to tell me that the car was a police car.

The disinterest disappeared from her eyes and fear replaced it. She crouched near the doorway and I crouched beside her, scarcely less afraid. The footsteps became louder and she edged nearer to me. Clearly *any* human could give her comfort from the thought of inevitable discovery.

Long shadows appeared in the doorway, the heat of the day urging the sweat of fear as it coursed down my forehead. Feet could now be seen approaching and... But the policemen did not enter, continuing on past the shelter... Past the old fence that skirted the allotments and on to the copse which stood on their border where I had originally found the photographs.

The girl looked into my face as if searching for a reason. I had to show her. I took her to the entrance and we watched while the policemen searched the ground, hitting at the undergrowth as they did so.

And, as they returned I pulled her back into the safety of the entrance. She looked at me.

'You knew,' she said, mistaking my smile of reassurance. Outside the grumbling voices of the policemen became audible. 'Bloody kids and their stories,' said one.

'Last time we listen to a kid. Bloody laughing stock we'll be.'

' "Find your dirty pics then chief?" I can hear it now. Only really dirty pics in Essex are in the nick being studied to see whether prosecutions should be brought.

'And the only people affected by them are Lander and Smiley who have to have ten minutes in the shower before they can stand behind the desk again.'

The other policeman laughed, and they returned to the car and drove away.

The girl looked at me. Then she threw her arms around me and kissed me. If she needed any convincing that I had removed the photographs in order to destroy them - and thereby save her from the shame of discovery - then the existence on my person of a box of matches did little to hinder my cause. I withdrew these and motioned towards the photographs, but the girl's hand restrained me.

'Did you admire me so much?'

'Loved. I loved you.'

She smiled:

'Yes I believe you; I don't know whether you told the police to put them off the scent once you had moved them. It seems unlikely. Too elaborate.'

I nodded.

'But you meant to save me?'

I nodded again. I would cheerfully have used the matches to light faggots beneath my feet if I could save her again. But this rather extravagant sacrifice proved unnecessary.

The girl unclipped her bra and left the straps hanging:

'You shall have your show,' she said, and proceeded to tenderly pull the bra cups away from her breasts.

It was all so different from the mechanical acts of a few moments before. She caressed her breasts. And then she unclipped her suspenders. The modern man enjoys no delight such as the removal of stockings. I watched spellbound, glad nevertheless that she now appeared oblivious to my existence, performing to herself.

She peeled her stockings down those creamy legs and flung them to the far side of the shelter.

Then she laid her spread hands beside her breasts, down her body and, with her face looking upwards in a gesture of ecstasy, inside the elastic of her panties.

Down, down until her finger tips appeared at the lower end. The panties were so brief that she could hook her thumbs into the elastic and, with the air of a girl relieving herself of a tiresome necessity, slid the garment down her legs. With an orgasmic sigh she revealed a little fluffy ball of golden hair and turned - as if to hide it - but actually to exhibit her beautifully rounded bottom.

Suddenly, as the panties fell to her ankles and she whipped them away, she was anxious to be doing. She crouched by the stack of photographs and motioned for me to start the fire.

We packed them around with stones although the chance of the fire spreading was negligible. And all the time I worked her naked body was there, crouched beside me. I could smell it; I was so aware of it but I could no more touch it than I could say good morning to the queen.

The conflagration passed all too quickly. And she moved to where her clothes had been spread around. I watched her as she stooped to retrieve them. For a moment, she stood, looking at me.

'One last look,' she said, and then she began to dress. Strangely it was an act as intimate as her undressing. I felt it a compliment to me that she did not withdraw to do it. I watched spellbound until, her dress completed to her satisfaction, she stood ready to leave.

'Thank you,' she said - and kissed me. 'He was in such a panic he would not go near the photographs after he had dumped them. He thought the police would be waiting for him. I think his idea was to destroy them in small consignments. It needed a small boy to do the thing properly.'

She laughed: 'It needed someone brave,' she said, and kissed me lightly on the cheek. 'I have no need to be afraid any more.'

From that moment she seemed to forget me. She walked out of the shelter pausing only for a perfunctory wave. I wondered if I should see her again.

I walked back into the shelter and watched the last embers of the fire. I realised I should have to wait until all sign of it had gone and bury the ashes. There would be nothing left to incriminate her - or remind me.

I walked around the shelter which had been like a home for so long and decided I should dedicate it to her, my beautiful goddess. Then I discovered her panties, caught on a ledge in one corner.

At first I thought of running after her. Then I checked. It was not a garment one forgot to put on. The girl had clearly left them deliberately. I pressed them to my face and kissed them.

They were all that remained of the girl who had occupied my every waking thought - and haunted my dreams.

THE END